Moonflowers And Nightshade

A Sapphic Horror Anthology

Edited by Samantha Kolesnik

Table of Contents

Little Red Friend
Jade Lancaster

Each dawn, from my window, I watched a little red bird hop along the spine of a tree. There were moments of peace at this hour when the sky still bled copper. Before She knocked.

Flicking its tail feathers, the bird plucked berries from the spindles. They often toppled from its beak and splotches of squashed fruits cut through the grey path below. I leaned forward to watch him, pressing my fingers against the cool glass. Then, footsteps. I snagged the curtains closed and crawled below the bed covers, my head hitting the pillow just as the locks snapped.

Then She was there, bringing in flickering candlelight, her white skirts rasping across the wood. When She set down the breakfast tray, the porcelain warbled. The usual: a bowl of something puce, resembling oatmeal, and sweetened with honey that took off the bitter edge. I swallowed. Feigned a smile for Her. "I'm not hungry today."

She laughed and brushed a hand along her apron. "You need to eat."

I opened my mouth to argue, but Her lingering gaze made the words roll back into my belly, so I nodded and reached for the steaming bowl. I had to scrape off the layer of film before I could think about eating it. She waited.

1

Hazel gaze un-blinking. Her thin mouth puckered until I took the first mouthful.

"Have you forgotten the rules?" She asked.

"What rules?" I said, looking away from the sludge.

Her attention had moved to the window, where a slither of sunshine dribbled through the gap I'd left.

"You're not to snoop out of the window, Alma."

"I didn't."

"Stop lying! If I catch you poking around the window again, I am going to shutter it up. Do you understand?"

I nodded.

"Do you understand?"

"Yes."

And with that, she pulled together the curtains and blotted out the daylight.

"Good. Now eat." She crossed back toward me with a raised arm, but as I scrunched away, a soft pat landed on my head. "Eat."

When she left, the bolt slid across the door and the metal rang out cold and hollow behind her. Gathering the blankets in my fists, I pulled at them until I shook out all my rage.

When I left bed to pull back the curtains, my little red friend had gone.

In the morning, I stayed twisted under the sheets until the knock came. She brought up pale sludge that wriggled down my throat. Even though She lingered until I finished the bowl, She didn't bolt the door behind her. Once Her footsteps were faint, I hurried to the window, almost tripping on my nightdress, but behind the curtains, the crooked oak stood empty. I sucked in a breath that made my ribs creak and threw open the window, letting in air that smelled like rotting tree-roots and sunshine.

After each breakfast, I searched for my little red friend. Every draw of the curtain gentler, as if the wrinkling cloth might startle him, but every morning was a birdless stump. Instead, my time became filled with sketches in charcoal— my imagining of him wilting until he was nothing but a stick on a line.

One morning, when the sky was bruised and swollen with clouds, there was a girl. Skinny, with long hair like fire. She was grasping a cluster of lilies and extended her arm to every passerby, but they strolled on, pulling their coats tighter around them.

Kneeling on the windowsill, I watched her until the last light dwindled. She sold two. One white. One red. And when she tired of this street, she glanced up, her dark gaze meeting mine. With a gasp, I backed off into the shadows to blow out the candle.

The next afternoon, she came again, and she'd added white roses to her assortment. Her cheeks were gaunt, but her amber eyes were warm and beautiful. I smiled and this time, when she looked, I didn't back away.

"You don't get to stare at me all day and not buy a flower!"

I pulled open the window and leaned forward, grasping hard at the frame. "A flower. I don't have any money to buy a flower."

"Then maybe don't stare at me, little bird."

I frowned and slinked back from the ledge. I wanted to tell her to go somewhere else then, but my words couldn't find my mouth and so, I snagged the curtains shut.

"I brought you a gift!" She cried, flinging open the door. I sat cross-legged in the corner wearing a blanket and used my foot to shove the drawing of the flower girl under the bed. "Oh?" The charcoal rattled against the floorboards and I wiped the black off against my dress.

She carried in a tall black cage, where terrified squeaks erupted from somewhere burrowed beneath paper shavings. "Happy Birthday!"

"A mouse?" I asked, rubbing my nose.

"Rats!" She replied, setting down the cage. "I hope you appreciate it. You know sneaking things into this house isn't easy."

I stared for a long moment before looking back up and forcing a smile. "Thank you."

She grinned, and with Her sleeve, rubbed away the smear on my nose before quietly leaving.

The three rats were ugly things, with tiny red eyes, and the smell of their piss burned my nose. But there was something about them, rummaging through paper and their little teeth gnawing at the bars, that I liked. Something that made me feel less alone. They knew what it was to be trapped. To want only for food and freedom. I watched them for hours, pushing my face up against the cold metal. Spoke to them softly, so they'd get used to my voice. At night, I let them out, and the sound of their scratching nails lulled me to sleep.

Little Red Friend

The red-haired girl came back almost daily now. Today, I stood with the skinniest rat squirming between my fingers. Like always, the window was open, just in case she had something to say.

"Hello rat-girl. Do you have any money yet?" Her flower bundle was drooping a little, cheeks growing gaunter. These days, the streets were quiet, and as the autumnal breeze swept in, her summer flowers began to rot.

"Soon." I tried to force a smile.

"You know, rat-girl, I am starting to think you're a liar," she said, plucking at a rose. The petals had turned wine-red and she'd tied thin pink ribbons around the stems to spruce them up. I cleared my throat.

"I suppose I should really move on to another part of town. I hear White Square has rich men with sympathetic wives."

"Wait!" I grabbed at the window frame and tried to swallow the shaking from my voice. The rat scuttled further up my arm and sat on my shoulder. "Wait..."

She cocked a brow. "I'm waiting."

"White Square is full of snobs, you'll never sell any flowers," I said.

"Is that so?" she asked, leaning against the lamppost.

I relaxed my shoulders. "That's so! You know, I've even heard there's an outbreak of the pox 'round that way. The kind that makes your skin blister with yellow pus. I've seen men from White Square in top hats and tails with rotting flesh, you know?"

She let out a chirp of laughter then, one that made her shoulders shake. "Well, rat-girl, it's a risk I'm willing to take, seeing as the people of this little town don't want to buy my flowers. I'd rather have pus-filled blisters than starve."

I huffed at the new nickname and gingerly reached up to stroke a finger along my new pet's spine. "If I had money, I'd buy your flowers."

"But you don't."

"Maybe I can get you some food instead?"

She paused. Her grip on the flowers tightened. "Okay rat-girl. If you can get me some food, maybe I'll come back."

I smiled. "I have a name you know. It's Alma."

After sunset, I waited by the door, until the hallway light was snuffed out. Out there, floorboards creaked and at last, Her bedroom door closed. I twisted the doorknob to my room slowly, *slowly*, so it made the faintest sigh when it opened. The hallway still smelled like candle wax, and behind Her door, Her bed frame creaked.

Taking in a breath, I tip-toed into the hall, and descended the stairs sideways, reaching out my foot to test for soft spots in the slats before stepping onto them. On the last step, a quiet groan rattled beneath me and I startled, waiting for the rumblings above my head. But when no footsteps came, I took the final step onto the cool stone floor.

Moonlight pooled in through the kitchen window. I had to feel for the counters, fingers trailing the wood until I found the bread box. Reaching inside, the sourdough was soft, and the smell was divine. I took a bite from the loaf, ripping off the crust with my teeth and spilling crumbs down my nightdress. And then another bite.

Sinking my thumbs into the loaf, I split it open in the middle and bit into the soft part. The loaf crumbled in my hands until I was left with a few ragged pieces. I swallowed and wiped at my mouth. Snagging the tea towel off the stove, I wrapped up the scraps, along with a lump of cheese and tucked them away before I could think of devouring the rest.

Once I was safely upstairs, I tucked the flower girl's bread away inside my top drawer, and when I slept, I dreamt of her amber eyes.

"Where is it?"

I shot up in bed, my heart trilling in my chest. Before I could string back together my consciousness, She asked again.

"Where is it, Alma?" And She yanked at my covers, exposing my feet to the chill.

"Where's what?"

"You know perfectly well what! The bread! You stole an entire loaf of bread?"

I snatched at the covers, but She pulled again and they unraveled from my grasp. My thoughts clattered like dominoes. Tell Her the truth, tell Her I was hungry, tell Her it wasn't me. Tell Her what? And so, my mouth rattled like a voiceless puppet before she cut through.

"I clothe you. I feed you. I keep you hidden away in here so you don't die out there on the streets and this is what you do? You steal from them?" She threw her arms up in defeat. "What if you were seen, Alma? What then? Then it would be us both on the streets!"

I wanted to tell Her I was sorry. But I wasn't.

She paced the room, heels clapping against the wood, her expression reeling. "I don't have time for your lies, Alma. I have to fix them breakfast and you right now… you are just going to have to wait until I decide what I'm going to do with you."

Her arms trembled and for a moment, I thought She might unleash Her rage. Instead, She strutted out and both bolts rattled across the door. She didn't come back with breakfast.

When my body wavered like this, the coolness of the wood pulled my heart back down from my head. I lay with my cheek pressed onto the floor and traced my hand along the grains. They felt nice under my fingers.

A quiet rustling came from behind. I rolled over to see tiny feet scuttle under my bed. "Hello little man," I said, reaching my arm beneath the frame to try and touch him. "You must be hungry too, uh?"

He stayed tucked at the back, body all puffed up with anxiety. I knew just the thing. I crawled out to retrieve the little seed mixture from the drawer and returned to lay on my stomach and scatter a handful of them. Ruffling his nose, whiskers twitching, he moved closer until he was right by my side, grasping at the food. I reached out to stroke his head. It felt nice to have a friend.

"Hey! Rat-girl!" The flower girl's voice was distorted from afar, but I scrambled from under the bed and flung open the window to let her know I was here. "Shuush. You're too loud." Her flowers were wilted now, the leaves brittle and yellowed but she looked beautiful, with her red hair piled on top of her head and her rouge-stained cheeks.

My face was suddenly hot and the hollow pit in my stomach didn't seem to hurt anymore.

"Hello," I said.

Her smile crinkled as far as the corners of her eyes. "Did you bring it?"

"Oh…" I looked over my shoulder at the drawer and swallowed. "I couldn't find much." When I looked back, that crinkle-eyed smile had washed away like chalk.

"But wait!" I rushed to get the bundle tucked away inside the drawer and my stomach groaned. "I got what I could!"

Her smile returned then and I made fast work, tying the cloth around the bread so it didn't slip out of the bundle. "I nearly got hurt getting this, you know," I flashed her my best heroic grin.

"Oooh, you are brave. All for me, too? Sweetheart, I'm flattered."

"Don't embarrass me," I laughed and flung the bundle out the window. "Tallyoooh," I cried, watching the package soar through the sky like a bird, and she snatched it from the air before it could hit the ground.

As she opened it, I leaned to get a better look, my cheeks burning hotter now. "Hey, I didn't get your name yet. What is it?"

"Is that all you got?"

"Uh."

She stared at the torn pieces of bread inside the bundle and looked back up at me, those pretty eyes narrow.

"It's all I could get. I'll try again another time but the doors are locked and…and if the Lord of the house notices that things are going missing, the housekeeper…my friend…She could get us kicked out…"

"It's okay…"

I never knew my heart could feel like a worm and it slithered slowly into my gut. "I'm sorry."

She twirled a flower stem between her finger and thumb. "I was expecting a little more, seeing as I'm giving you a flower and all."

I tipped my head. "Why don't you come back tomorrow? I…She has to unlock the door sometime."

She blew out a sigh and shook her head. "No, no. It's okay. Like I said, White Square. That's the place where I can probably make something more. It was nice knowing you though, rat-girl."

"Hey, I can trade! You're hungry, right? I can offer…I can…" I turned to look around the room and at what else I had tucked away. One of the rats—the squirmy grey one— scuttled past, so I grabbed him in my fist. It squeaked, tiny claws fraying the fabric of my dress. "Have him! Have him. You can eat him." My face flushed.

A smile rippled across her face. "Okay. Throw it." She dropped the flowers and held out her cupped hands, raising them for the rat.

"No. Wait…"

"Throw it, rat-girl."

I hesitated, the rat's tail flicking against my wrist as it tried to pry from my grasp.

The flower girl lifted her chin. "Please. I'm so hungry."

I blew out my cheeks and hurried to the bed to drag out a little wooden box. I shut the squeaking rat inside and with a long piece of ribbon, lowered him out of the window on my makeshift pulley, the fragile box spinning as it descended. The girl smiled and after unfastening the box, tied a rose to the flapping piece of ribbon. It dangled, upside down as I pulled it back up. My cheeks burned scarlet as I clutched it to my chest. When I looked back to thank her, she was sinking her teeth into my squirming rat's stomach and its guts splattered over her lips.

When I got into bed, I cried until my throat burned. I pulled the covers over my head and sobbed hard, hoping the blankets might muffle my cries, and hoping She didn't hear me. My stomach hurt. I wasn't going to speak to the flower-girl again.

I stayed there, limbs coiled tightly until there was a soft knock at my door. Cold metal snapped back, and the door groaned when it opened. "I brought you some soup."

"Thank you," I whispered, and waited until the door clicked back. Kale soup, with wilted leaves floating at the surface. My stomach ached with hunger, but I couldn't bring myself to touch the soup.

When the rose petals had turned brown and wrinkled, I plucked the ribbon from the stem and fastened it into a bow in my hair. That day, the flower-girl returned. Her blooms were brighter today. Ruffled petals in bursts of pink. Foxgloves hung like strings of bells over her arms. I leaned out from behind the curtain and when she looked up, I hid from view.

"Hey rat-girl!"

I huffed and pressed my shoulders against the wall.

"You look pretty with that ribbon in your hair!"

My cheeks burned again.

"I have a flower for you, you know! To say thanks."

I peeked back around and there she was, twirling a rhododendron in her fingers. I stepped out and wrinkled my nose. "I don't want it."

She smiled and shook out the petals. "Have you gone all shy on me, now?"

"No!"

Her brows knitted together and the flower drooped, hanging upside down in her grasp. "Ah. I upset you last time, hm? I'm sorry."

Something rippled through me, a sensation that made my insides twist. I ran my fingers along the windowsill, scratching at the paint in the wood until it flaked under my nails. "No. I'm sorry, I didn't mean to be rude."

She laughed, a sweet sound. I wanted to hear her laugh again.

"I know you didn't, rat-girl. So, will you take the flower?"

I nodded and pulled at the window. The frame squeaked from the tug. Thrusting my arms outside, I wiggled my fingers, ready to grasp at the stem. These types of flowers didn't have thorns, but if they did, I'd brave a sliced finger in exchange for her laugh.

"No. You have to come down for it."

I snorted and pushed my palms flat against the sill. "How? I'd fall."

She made a grand gesture toward the lead pipe that ran alongside the window.

I shook my head.

"Oh come on, rat-girl!"

12

Behind me, the staircase creaked. She must have been coming upstairs with more kale soup. "No. No, I can't. She'll see! I'll be in trouble."

"She keeps you locked up in here. Is that what you want for the rest of your life? Come with me. Let's go to White Square!" Her eyes grew wild at the thrill of the idea and she dropped her bouquets by her feet and took a quick step forward.

"I'll fall!" I peered over the edge at the drop and my breath rattled. In the hallway, Her footsteps grew louder. It had to be now. It had to be now. I imagined what it would be like, our fingers woven together as we strolled through White Square to a backdrop of violin music and my hair, warmed by sunshine. I could eat bread until my stomach swelled and ached with it. No more pale mush for breakfast. I could be happy.

The flower-girl grasped at the lead pipe and scrambled up, her feet scuffing against the bricks. "Come on, it's okay. I won't hurt you," and she stretched out her arm toward me. I leaned further out of the open window, grasping harder at the frame, and swung one of my legs over. And, with my leg dangling over the ledge, my heart felt like a rock and I swore I was going to fall from the sheer weight of it.

"Come on!" She said and pushed up on a rock to gain purchase, her fingers wriggling toward me. Her pale face became gaunter in the shadows. "Come on, rat-girl!"

Her tone was biting and I hesitated for a moment, trying to make sense of the expression that knitted her brows together.

"My name is Alma!" I cried, and swung my leg back over the windowsill and into the bedroom. The girl screamed—a lung-piercing sound that made goosebumps like razors along my back.

The skin on her face rippled, and her wide-eyed stare turned yellow. When she grabbed my ankle, her talons ripped a tear through my skin and blood dripped down my feet. I shrieked and pulled back, but her claws sunk deeper, and she dragged me back over the window ledge.

My flailing arms scrambled to find something to grab, but her strength snapped my leg. The flare of pain that followed turned my scream acidic.

Her head snapped back and there was a mighty pop as her jaw dislocated. Her mouth opened into a gash that grew wider and she was pulling me into it, legs first. The heat of her breath against my skin made my stomach churn and then a cool hand gripped mine. She was there at the window pulling my arms with such force, I thought they were going to pop from their sockets. Her face twisted in anguish. "Alma!"

"Please!" I cried back, my slippery hand clutching Hers. But Her arms were weak, and I dangled above the monster's mouth like a fish on a hook. I tried to kick up into its mouth but it was too big, and my broken leg couldn't swing so high. "Please! Flower girl. I thought you were my friend." I looked up at those yellow-eyes, my own swollen with tears and she hissed. Her breath sprayed water droplets over my dress. "You're nothing but a rat," she replied, voice low and serpentine.

"Please!" I cried. Her bristled tongue leapt out and hooked around my waist.

The housekeeper screamed, Her grasp tightening. But the monster wrenched me into its mouth and our fingers were parted. I stared up at Her terrified face and then,

14

darkness. A slippery wetness enveloped me so tightly, I couldn't scream. And then she bit down. My ribs crushed beneath the strength of its teeth, and I tumbled, down, down into the emptiness of its belly. Before my light was snuffed out, I heard the terrifying twitter of a little bird.

Common Oleander

Rae Knowles

Oleander reigns the undisputed queen of the garden. Her five-fingered pink blossoms sprawl above the white tufts of flowering water hemlock and his cousin, white snakeroot. *Not cousin*, Becca always reminds me, but I am more vulnerable to aesthetics and less interested in genus and species. I prefer to think of them as not-so-distant relations, parted for many years and now reunited, here in our yard.

I watch Becca. She's sitting cross-legged, leaves swaying on sprawling stems about her cheeks. Breezes entangle them in her natural blonde hair, which flows freely. She prunes by hand.

I used to worry. When she saw my wide eyes the first time I caught her pinching off yellow leaves with her fingernails, she giggled.

"Isn't that—"

"You have to eat it, sweetie," she'd said.

Now we pass the morning hours here. I, with my steaming tea in the wicker chair, and she, still in her nightgown, barefoot amidst her flora. This is our spring routine.

"Castor bean's unhappy," she says. Her mouth tightens and my guts twitch. "You'll run into town, won't you? Pick up some bananas for the PH?"

"Of course." I sigh. An easy fix. When the spider mites came last year, it wasn't so simple. I spent weeks tiptoeing around her volatile mood.

"And don't let Betsy see you." A given. She plucks seeds from the castor bean. Dirt has blackened the soles of her feet. "When will our visitor arrive?"

"Soon."

Rolling hills surround us on all sides, dotted by off-white cottages so much like our own. Most of the neighbors prefer their views unrestricted, but our five acres are bordered by a simple wooden post fence. It's not enough to keep the foxes from wandering in, or the stray dogs. In fact, it's mostly ceremonial, but the twists of barbed wire around the entry tell the odd salesman or religious zealot, *you are most unwelcome*. And for us, that is enough.

Uncut grasses sway over the landscape, an ocean of billowing green. My eyes scan the horizon, trace our simple fence, return to Becca, then follow the garden to its limit, where the freshly dug soil wriggles with earthworms. Seeds in hand, she takes her seat beside me, wicker threads bending with her weight. Unfurling her palm, she lifts them to my face for inspection.

"Despite the rich burgundy leaves, castor seeds are cool tone brown, specked in heterogeneous patterns." She points one out. "This one's spotted like a leopard."

This close, I can smell her intoxicating mix of lavender soap and organic earth.

"Looks like a beetle to me."

She smirks, and her amber eyes meet mine. Smoothing back a wisp of my hair, her finger traces my earlobe. "Gem—"

My insides collapse. She knows my name on her lips makes me swoon.

"Let's just sit here a while."

Blood rushes to my cheeks.

"At least until our guest arrives."

Five years together and still I find myself completely disarmed by her. Woefully enchanted. "Of course, baby." I lean in, as she knew I would, and her eyes gently close, her chin tilting upward. My lips sink into her supple kiss. Her tongue skims the ridges of my teeth, and I'm lost until she pulls away.

"Can I see it?"

Her brow arches, and I take her by the hand. Through the living web of bushes and vines, she trails me. Our small shed doesn't hold much: the wheelbarrow, spare hose, seedling trays, and it needs another coat of periwinkle paint, but inside I show her I'm prepared. Bags of woodchips and sawdust piled atop one another earn me a beaming grin and the feeling of her arms around my waist.

"The nitrogen mixes with the carbon and makes a happy home for microbes," she begins to explain again, holding me tight.

"I know, I remember."

The distant sputtering of an engine draws our attention to the one-lane road.

"Is that him?" she asks, as if I could know for sure.

Muted red, the truck rises above a hilltop then slopes back down, out of sight. It winds through the gentle curves, the melody of a country song riding in on a breeze as it draws closer.

"Go put the tea on," she says.

By the time he knocks, the water has warmed, and Becca has stepped into the shower. I remove the kettle from the burner, and twirl the spiraling steam. I let him loiter on the porch until he knocks a second time. I spy through the peephole. He's a few years older than he said, his dark hair shot through with gray. It must have been an old picture. He shifts his weight, taps on his jeans and rubs his palm over a tear in the denim.

"Who is it?" I ask through the door.

His eyes roll. "Paul. Paul Richards? Aren't you expecting me?" Hairline wrinkles form between his unkempt brows.

"Paul Richards?" I pretend to confirm. I understand using a false name, but he could've put a bit more thought into his pseudonym.

"Maybe I have the wrong—"

I open the door. His tank top looks even more faded and pitiful without the peephole's distortion. He scratches at his belly where it bulges over his pants.

"I'm here about the groundskeeper position. Do I have the wrong house?"

Not in the way you mean, I think.

"Of course." I put on my hostess smile. "Come on in, I've just made a pot of tea."

I usher him to the couch where he wavers before he sits, as if sitting on the rose pattern might somehow diminish his masculinity. Pouring us each a cup of tea, I settle in the loveseat. Vapors from my cup waft around my nose and I take in the floral scent. He gulps his down in two swallows.

"I've forgotten the trail mix! You must think I'm a lousy host." I nestle my cup on its matching saucer and return to the kitchen, feeling his impatience on my back. On his lap I place a bowl of pretzels, candies, nuts, and other goodies. He tosses a handful into his irritated grimace.

"It's all cash, right?" he says through chomps, peppering the air with bits of chewed nuts.

"That's right."

The water turns off.

"Becca will be with us in just a moment."

"Who?"

"She likes to be part of the interviews."

He nods and leans back against the sofa cushions. His legs spread, knees squaring with his shoulders now that he's comfortable. Becca calls them guests or visitors, but I think of them as candidates. They are, after all, here to fill a vacant role. I've found through experience that offering cash brings in a particular type of man, the type with reasons not to use his real name. Becca doesn't get hung up on these sorts of things. She's all about results. But I prefer it this way.

"Do you live in town?" I ask, though I know the answer.

"Yeah," he lies. "Not far."

I nod. In a town of four hundred, it's easy to know when you're talking to an outsider. He pulls his phone from his pocket, the flip kind. I guess I'm boring him.

"Is it nostalgia?" Becca asks, parading out of the bedroom. She's put on a sundress, vivid yellow pansies against white cotton.

Our candidate sports a puzzled look. Not an ironic hipster then.

"Follow me to the garden." Becca takes long strides out the French doors. Her speed lifts the hem of her dress, giving a tantalizing view of her upper thigh. I watch him stare. She talks maintenance work, but his eyes focus on her lips. I stand beside her, and rub her shoulder while she speaks.

"You two sisters?" he asks.

I don't try to hide the pang of anger. In a larger city, I think my short hairstyle would offer a clue. But here in the Meadowland it's just as common on the hetero farmers' wives.

"This is common oleander," she explains, drifting from my side and gazing at the pink blossoms like a paramour. "But I think you'll agree there's nothing common about mine."

He steps between Becca and me.

Her hand hovers over the delicate petals. "You must never touch them. The sap can cause rashes for some people. Not me." She plucks a single bloom, tucks it behind her ear.

"What's this one," he asks, feigning interest as he motions toward the wide leaves of our tobacco patch.

"That one you can touch." *Touch* pulls her mouth into a seductive O shape.

Beads of sweat form at his hairline. I sit in my wicker chair.

"Funny thing about tobacco. Even children know that smoking it will kill you, but far less know that the faster death comes if you eat the leaves."

He glances over, sizing me up, letting her words fall into the background.

"And this one," she goes on, "rosary pea. People make jewelry from the seeds, which are perfectly harmless intact."

A droplet rolls down his temple. He bites at his cheek.

"But they contain abrin. So any jewelry makers with pricked fingers and cracked seeds have a painful few days of organ failure before their death."

He snorts. "Lucky for me, I don't make jewelry."

She nods. "I'm sure you know about castor bean."

"Can't say I do."

"It only takes two seeds to kill a child. More for an adult."

His hand clutches at his stomach. I hear it grumble and flip from twenty feet away.

"How much trail mix did you say you ate?"

He retches, and his skin turns a shade of gray. Stumbling off the path, he dry heaves.

"White snakeroot killed Lincoln's mother. And water hemlock, believe it or not, is in the carrot family."

Both hands clutch at his abdomen. His shoulders quake.

"People sometimes confuse it with celery or parsnips. But considering the cicutoxin, it's the last mistake they tend to make."

He stumbles to his knees. She points around the garden, one plant at a time.

"Cicutoxin, atropine and scopolamine, tremetol, ricin—I'm sure you've heard of that one—abrin, anabasine," she floats back to the queen—precious oleander. "And oleandrin, of course."

Thick vomit pours from his mouth. It collects on his chin in chunks.

"You didn't get that one though. I couldn't bear to sacrifice even a cutting of it. Not this close to the festival."

The realization comes to him, and his surprise mixes with rage. He crawls toward her, lashing out with wild hands. She steps backward, easily avoiding his flailing limbs.

"Vomiting, diarrhea, convulsions. Most of the toxins have a similar effect, which I'm sure you can attest to now."

A seizure rocks his body. Thin foam drizzles from his mouth.

"Shouldn't be long now."

A gurgling groan emits from his throat as he makes his last stand. To my shock, he regains his footing, and I see my own fear reflected in Becca's eyes. He catches hold of her and I dash around the side of the house to grab our rusty shovel. Tiny splinters wedge into my unprotected palms as I dig my fingernails into the wooden handle for grip. When I clear the corner, he's taken her to the ground, punching wildly about her head.

Bone cracks as the metal spade makes contact, and Becca rolls his stunned body off hers. She staggers to her feet, and I bring the shovel down over his bleeding head again and again, unwilling to take any chances. His skull reduced to mush, I toss the tool aside. Becca takes her place by my side, and a few drops of blood spill from her nose.

"What a shame."

Common Oleander

My heart skips at the sound of Betsy's voice. Becca goes pale. We both turn toward the north end of the property, and there she is, leaning on the fence post, peering at us beneath the wide brim of her church hat.

Becca wipes her nose with the back of her arm, leaving a streak of burnt orange on her upper lip.

Betsy motions toward the garden and we see it. Broken stems, fallen flowers, scattered leaves. A man-sized indent where his tackle flattened the nightshade patch. Becca falls to her knees. Her eyes water as the battered stems drape limply around her grasp.

"Looks like you'll have to start over from seeds." There's a smug quality to her tone.

I retort. "Unfortunately for you, the oleander is untouched."

Betsy crinkles her nose. "No matter. My champion blooms speak for themselves every year at the festival. This year will be no different."

Becca dusts off her knees and sulks inside, mourning the loss of her brood.

"Go tend to them, then," I insist.

She smirks. "I shall." Sneaking one last glance at the candidate's broken body, she adds, "You'd better get going anyhow. You've got your work cut out for you today I see."

Plodding away through the long grasses, she leaves a depressed trail of folded stalks in her wake. Despite my disdain for her, I know she's right. Disarticulating his body will consume me through nightfall. I know better than to try to comfort Becca. She is, no doubt, back under the scalding shower, calculating the time it will take to regrow her nightshade to the fullness and luster of the decimated patch.

25

I spend hours stripping away the flesh, unwinding the tendons, and sawing through bones. Clotted blood soaks into the earth and it saturates the ground. I've finally got him into manageable pieces. I relocate his hands, disconnected at the wrist—his shins, detached at the knee and ankle—and feet, to perfectly-sized holes around the garden. I lay his pieces atop woodchips and sawdust, and cover them up with thick layers of soil. The largest hole is reserved for the torso, so heavy I have to drag it. Becca doesn't help with this part. She never does. We each have our role, our spring routine. When he's firmly planted, the sun is dipping beneath the horizon, staining the green hills orange. I return to the house, a collection of wildflowers in hand. It's a small offering to soothe Becca's loss. Wordlessly, she puts them in water.

"Is it true, you think?" Her lip quivers.

My arm circles her hips. I lead her to the couch, and she settles beside me.

"Betsy may have a winning streak, but she was supplementing long before we moved here. We've got to give it time."

Becca shakes her head, and stares at the seam where the wall meets the hardwood.

"It's the realtor's fault. He should've mentioned the loamy soil. If we'd have known—"

I pull her into my embrace before she can spiral. It's easier to blame. Even if we didn't garden then or know about the Meadowland Festival.

"The Hendricks are judging this year. Betsy knows they haven't liked her since the incident with the goats. She came over here to taunt us just to boost her fragile ego, old coot."

Common Oleander

Becca sniffs and composes herself with fragile hope. "Do you really think we have a shot?"

I gaze into the depths of her amber eyes. "Your oleanders are stunning, my love. World class. And by May, our visitor will be feeding them, boosting their luscious bouquets. I wouldn't be surprised if we got magenta hues."

I weave my fingers into the waves of her hair. Her soft breath warms my chest. Tomorrow I'll make tea. Becca will wander barefoot into the garden and prune bushes by hand in her nightgown. I'll watch from my wicker chair.

This is our spring routine.

Fingers

E.F. Schraeder

"Tell me, do you think it's people getting close to you, or being close to them that bothers you most?" Dr. Fields leaned forward with her elbows on her knees.

Classic therapy. Answer a question with another question. "I don't know, Dr. Strangelove. What do you think?"

"Very funny, Maya. I'm being serious. First, I could do without the nickname. And second, I really want to know what you think."

"I think most Americans hate women. That doesn't make being a lesbian very easy."

"Okay, but I don't want to talk about politics. I want to hear what you think about your fear of intimacy." Dr. Fields sat back in her chair. "Without the eyerolls, please."

"You don't think they're related? Even saying a nice word about a woman, especially if it's not about how she looks, begins with an apology, like you need some kind of excuse. To love something society hates. Well damn. Every single date, no matter how lousy, is a tiny act of revolution. There are more barriers than you can imagine to love like mine. I'm not sure if it's me or the world I'm afraid of."

"Of course. But why do you think it's hard for you to let people in? Are you afraid of physically being close?

29

Afraid to open yourself up to rejection? Or more afraid of being loved?"

Maya shrugged. "Honestly, I'll have to get back to you on that."

"Do you let yourself say yes?" Her eyebrow raised. "Are you afraid to say yes?"

"No, I date. I say yes. Sometimes. A friend of mine set me up for a date tonight, in fact."

"Great! That's progress. Just putting yourself out there is an important step. I want you to keep an open mind while you're out tonight. Think about saying yes. Think about these sessions."

Maya cringed. "That'd be a romance-killer."

Dr. Fields chuckled. "I mean about the purpose they serve. Your goals. Not the content. Consider what a single act of openness means to you. Intimacy happens one step at a time."

"Isn't that a bumper sticker? Sorry, just kidding, I get it. Love can mediate the world's negativity. I really believe that. And I want to try to be open this time."

"Good. And think about what matters to you, what you want to find and how your expectations impact your experiences."

Maya nodded. "I'll let you know how it goes."

***

Looks didn't matter much to Maya. She always believed that real beauty was something to be discovered and mined from the deep details of a person—the imperfections, to be specific. Sensual, honest beauty hid in the strange, subtle mannerisms and quirks—in wrinkles around the eyes, or a lopsided smile. Those small expressions and glances that only one other person understood. That was real intimacy.

So Maya hadn't expected much to come from this, or from any first date. At best, she assumed they'd end up as drinking buddies. Her habit was keeping people at a distance. She had the shoulder women cried on; she wasn't the one they cried about. She'd gotten used to being the bookish friend, not the heartthrob. Usually, that was fine.

Then she met Alex.

When Maya arrived at Su City, she spotted Alex right away from the black scarf with the floral print. Her heart skipped a beat when Alex waved.

Holy shit.

Alex said to look for the scarf and described herself as forgettable. She definitely lied. There was nothing forgettable about Alex.

Alex was jaw-dropping—gorgeous in a way Maya hadn't considered possible for non-famous people. Flawless. As if a team of stylists prepped her for the night. Alex nearly sparkled, sitting there alone at the table. Alex balanced on the sharp edge of being put together so well that it was almost ostentatious. Her full black hair fell to the shoulders, framing an angular jaw and long neck. She sipped at something bright red in a martini glass, probably a campari and vodka cocktail. Her dangling earrings sparkled, catching the light.

She was impossible not to notice. Perched in the center of the room, she seemed utterly comfortable in a way that required confidence most people couldn't manage while drinking alone. But Alex looked content as hell, like she could have been stood up and still enjoyed a meal. Not that anyone would stand her up.

Certainly, Maya wouldn't. *Let's see how afraid of intimacy I am tonight.* She headed to the table, removed her jacket, and hung it on the chair. Alex rose slightly, tilting her glass. A mix of attraction and nervousness sent a thrill through Maya's body. Her ears went pink.

"Nice to meet you in real time," Alex said. Her voice was low and smooth. "Hope you don't mind I took the liberty of ordering."

"Well, Alex, I have to compliment you on the restaurant. I've never been here before." Maya raised a dark eyebrow, tilting her head to one side, and glancing around the dimly lit room.

A faint smile played on Maya's face as she sat down. Alex rested her chin in one hand and returned Maya's gaze.

Maya was captivated already. She hadn't even had a sip of wine and this already qualified as a better than average date.

Alex bit down on her lower lip in a way that looked half-shy and half-playful. Her unflinching, electric, dark-eyed stare pointed at Maya. *Electric.* Her bronze complexion glowed in the candlelight.

"New to sushi, or just Su City?" Alex asked. Gold flecks in the fabric of her black top glinted as she spread her arms out, palms up. A welcoming gesture.

Everything about her shimmers.

Maya hesitated, aware that admitting she was un-adventurous may be a turn off. She sucked in a short breath, then landed on honesty. "Both. I don't usually get across town in the evenings, and to be real with you, I hardly ever go out to dinner."

"Ah. I love to cook. Do you cook, Maya?"

Fingers

I'm not sure how that can sound flirty, but it does. Maya smiled. She loosened the navy tie from the grey striped shirt. She felt a little formal and too business-casual. She suddenly wished she'd stopped home to change clothes after work. *Mental note for next session with Dr. Fields, I did not feel like holding back.*

A plate arrived between them containing green rolls with sprigs of asparagus jutting out from rice.

Alex leaned forward. Beneath the table she crossed her ankles and nudged Maya's foot.

"I like it raw." Alex winked. "Welcome to the 21st century, honey. You're landing with honors." She reached her chopsticks across the table, a bite sized roll poised between them. She pressed the sushi to Maya's mouth.

The blend of salty soy sauce and wasabi burned her lips. Maya caught herself salivating. For the food, to be sure, but more than a little for Alex too. Her fingers stroked the chopsticks, and somehow it was like she was touching her. *Everywhere.* Her body hummed with a jolt of desire she hadn't felt in years. Maybe longer.

Maya took the sushi into her mouth. It was soft and moist, pure sensuality. She swallowed, then licked her lips. *Maybe wasabi burns fear away.*

"Pretty provocative for a first date move, isn't it?" Alex asked, running the empty chopstick along Maya's lower lip.

***

Maya didn't expect to go to bed with Alex that night, and she didn't. Not the night after either, but they kept meeting, again and again. Evenings only, always for dinner. And no matter how much she ate, Maya always left hungry for more. For weeks, they slipped away from routines and friends and pursued each other. Attraction became as palpable as a third guest at the dinner table.

"I think she likes to do things on short notice, you know? Maybe she's afraid of commitments. But honestly, Dr. Fields, for now that works for me." Maya smiled.

"Why do you think?"

"Well, I think it's less stressful, you know? I don't worry about how it's going. We just meet up when we can. It's low key. It's going really well. I'm really feeling good about her so far."

"Do you ever make plans?"

"No. We never spoke on the phone, either. We arrange dinners on the go."

"Sounds very impromptu. All via text?"

"It's reciprocal. Sometimes I invite her, sometimes the other way around. But it's been nice. She's not clingy at all like—"

"A lot of women you've been involved with?"

Maya nodded. "It's exciting. Alex is different. Flirty. Casual. Fun."

"I'm glad to hear you're letting yourself go with it. Keep saying yes."

"No doubt."

***

"I love this seating style, don't you," Alex asked. She cozied into a floor cushion at Abyssinia, the only Ethiopian restaurant downtown.

Maya nodded. She dipped some spongey injera into a bowl of spicy lentils, rolling the flatbread into a bite sized mouthful, and held it across the low table.

Alex leaned forward and opened her mouth. Her eyes flashed with something like lust, and a smile played on her face.

"This is my favorite indulgence," Maya said. She rested a thumb on Alex's lower lip while she chewed. Alex moaned in pleasure and Maya felt that quivering moan in her cells.

"So far." Alex opened her mouth again and took Maya's fingers in, caressing them with her tongue. "No utensils. Guess I need those fingers of yours."

They stared down at the scattered remnants of their meal. Dropped potatoes, carrots, and beans between the bowls of vegetables. Alex grabbed another piece of injera, rolled it into a tube, and took a bite. Maya's face flushed.

"Eating is rather like sex, don't you think?" Alex asked. "No matter how long it is between bites, you've got to have it eventually."

The idea of saying yes was getting easier with every meal. Maya leaned forward, elbows on the dark wooden table. Her knees jutted up, nearly to her ears.

Maya hesitated. "This may sound forward, but I may want to try you next."

Alex let out a cackling laugh that let the air out of the tension between them. "Be careful what you wish for."

"Why? Tell me we aren't just about food." For a moment, Maya worried she'd read the whole thing wrong. Maybe she was in the friend zone. She bit down on her lower lip, waiting for a reply.

Alex smiled, but said nothing.

The silence made Maya nervous. *Uncomfortable.* She bit so hard her lip hurt.

"Never mind," Maya said, her voice a whisper. She let out a quick breath. "I needed a dinner companion, sure. I enjoy our meals together, I just thought, I mean—." *Backpedaling. Welcome to the friend zone. Again.*

"We'll see."

Maya relaxed. Maybe they were taking it slow. Dr. Fields would approve of that. Either way, Maya enjoyed their time. And the meals they shared were nearly as steamy as sex. The intense flavors, the overpowering scents, exotic oils saturating the mouth. The near touches. Every meal with Alex took on the physicality of an orgasm. Exhilarating, sure, and more than a little exhausting.

***

"Do you think this food-play is a fetish?" Maya glanced down at her nails.

"I don't think you should try to label it. Are you still enjoying your time with her?" Dr. Fields set her notebook down and stared at Maya.

Maya looked up and nodded. "Yes. But her lukewarm response made me nervous, like she's maybe not as into me as I am."

"Do you feel rejected?"

"Well, that's the thing. I don't. We spend a lot of time together. We flirt like crazy. So no. I'm just going to hold back a little. I won't ask about going further than teasing for a while."

"It's still casual and impromptu?"

36

"Yes. And fun. Why push and risk losing what we have?"

"It's okay to go slowly. I'm glad to hear you're going with it. You're really letting yourself explore desire. It sounds like you're making progress."

***

But Maya's questions lingered. *Who was this woman? She gets me hot and leaves me cold at the end of the night. Why do I like it so much? Maybe I want to be let down, like Dr. Fields said a few months ago.*

Maya admired Alex's candid sexuality and confidence, even if it left her speechless, stunned, and often rather frustrated.

When Alex reached across the table, her hand hovered. Maya tensed, thinking she may be leaning forward for a kiss. *At last!*

Instead, Alex grabbed the check. "It's on me tonight," she said, rising.

The next night, Maya considered where to meet Alex next. Then an idea struck. She texted an invite of a different sort.

"7pm. Forest Park"

Relax into it. Enjoy the perpetual arousal. Her hands.

Maya spread a soft, blue flannel blanket on the ground and arranged containers of spiced olives, stuffed baby eggplants, red and green grapes, peeled blood orange wedges. She set out a bottle of red wine and carefully moved the items into a tight semicircle to ensure they'd have nowhere to sit but close together.

A picnic at dusk sends one message: this is a date.

The sounds of the park faded into a faint backdrop as the sun began to set, yet the outdoor air vibrated with life. This was far different than being in a dimly lit dining room, flirting and wishing. Here, Maya hoped the atmosphere would inspire a sudden honesty between them so they could really talk, maybe for the first time.

Alex arrived, a smile on her face. She scooted close to Maya, their shoulders brushing. They barely spoke as they settled in for their meal. Maya slid an orange wedge into her mouth. Alex nestled closer, picked up a slice, and rubbed it to Maya's lips. Soon the tangy juice seeped from the corner of Maya's mouth. Alex licked away a sticky drip, but never quite kissed her.

Maya moaned. "I don't mean to sexualize this, but I feel your tongue everywhere when you touch me."

Alex laughed. "Everywhere?"

Maya's cheeks flushed.

Alex smiled, setting a hand on Maya's thigh. "Oh, it's sexual. There's nothing hotter than wanting sex. Having it is so easy. And so often such a disappointment. But what you eat stays with you."

Maya's brow furrowed with an unasked question.

Alex toyed with Maya's mouth through the meal, caressing her lips and face. Tracing slender fingers along Maya's throat. The sensations sent electric spikes through her nerves.

Each bite tingled with thrills and her skin warmed under Alex's touch.

"You're like a fever," Maya said.

Desire peaked with each new mouthful of food they shared. Maya longed for Alex's hands to explore her body, but Alex held back.

Maybe Alex liked being in control. She was playful as hell, but so careful. Maya wondered when they'd get closer. *That was progress, all right.* For the first time in her life, she was the one who wanted more.

Alex's finger slipped along, then into Maya's parted lips. Maya shifted away, sitting up straight.

"No matter where we go, you'll go home each night, hungry for me, won't you?" Alex asked.

Maya nodded.

***

"It's beyond frustrating, Dr. Fields. I think I'm cured. Wherever this is headed, I'm on board."

"You're really blossoming. It doesn't sound like you're carrying any of your old baggage with this relationship. That's so exciting."

Dr. Fields didn't know the half of it.

***

"43 Elmore. Right now."

Maya stared at the phone. She didn't recognize the address, but she grinned, eager to see Alex again. She tapped the address and waited for the GPS to tell her where to go. She was far too infatuated to wonder where Alex would take her. She'd go anywhere Alex asked, no questions.

As Maya turned onto a residential street, she realized where she was headed. Alex's house. "Holy shit!" She slammed the steering wheel with an open palm. *So this was the night. Finally.* She glanced down at her attire, feeling more than a little pleased about the good choice in underwear. Black boy boxers and a ribbed tank were sexy without trying too hard. She parked her car in the driveway and practically ran to the door.

Alex's simple, beige bungalow with maroon shutters sat on a suburban street like a thousand others. Warm light beamed from inside, giving off a welcome glow.

Maya knocked twice.

"Come in. I'm almost done. Just one more ingredient," Alex called. Her voice was luscious and thick as velvet.

Maya opened the door and stepped inside. Somehow she'd expected something of a love dungeon from Alex, but no lacy undergarments hung from the lighting fixtures. No plush carpets. No incense. No music. Yet she wanted this woman more than anyone she'd ever met. Alex's very being was infused with sex. Desire flooded Maya like a drug, with a sweeping flush of heat that made her skin burn to be touched.

The fragrance of cinnamon hovered in the air. Maya's senses were overwhelmed with the scent. She glanced around the room, nervous and eager, then took a few steps into Alex's space. She ran a hand along a smooth, cool stone figure of two abstract beings locked in an embrace. *Some kind of fertility statue?* Even touching Alex's things turned her on.

I've just arrived, and I'm already on fire.

"Come into the kitchen," Alex called.

Maya followed the sound of her voice like she was in a trance. The scent of whatever was simmering grew stronger, pulling her like a magnet. When she entered the open kitchen, her eyes landed on Alex's back, on how the

40

slim fitting black tunic highlighted her curves. Maya bit her lower lip.

Alex didn't turn to face her. Instead she just kept stirring. Her elbow bent in a smooth, circular motion over a white enameled pan.

"Hungry?" Alex asked.

"More than you know," Maya said. Maya's stomach jumped and jolted. The sweet scent flooded her nostrils. She drank in Alex's environment, the warmth and intoxicating smells all luring her deeper. She felt closer to Alex than ever. The intimacy overwhelmed her—almost like a threat. *Don't be afraid to say yes.* She took another step toward Alex.

Alex turned to face Maya with a large black spoon in her hand. "Try this," she said, extending it. Alex eyed her as she moved closer.

Maya took in a mouthful of the red sauce. "Mmm. Tastes amazing. I'd like to pour it all over you." She licked her lips, trying to discern the odd blend of flavors settling on her palate. She pressed Alex against the stainless stove, but Alex wiggled an arm away, bracing herself at the counter.

"But be careful. It's hot." Alex smiled.

"It is hot." Maya pressed into her hips. "It's hot here, too," She nudged herself closer.

Alex clutched Maya's hand, pulling it onto the counter. In a swift motion, she struck it with a meat tenderizer.

"Ahh!" Maya screamed, yanking her hand away. Her hand bore painful, pointed marks. *What the hell?*

Alex placed a hand between Maya's legs and whispered. "Shh. I know what you want." She moved her fingers in at a slow, steady pace. She brought her other hand in front of Maya's face. Set a finger on her lips.

Stunned, Maya couldn't focus. The pain throbbed, but she was turned on as Alex's hand pinpointed just the right pace and pressure between her legs. Then she noticed the tip of Alex's finger. It was red.

Not just red. It was bleeding. With a small chunk missing.

Alex motioned to the pot on the stove. Blood seeped from the wound. "You like it?" She plunged the bloody finger into Maya's mouth. "You said you wanted to eat me next—"

Maya's sucked Alex's finger before she could stop herself, even as her eyes widened, realizing what she was doing. What she'd just consumed. The sauce.

It was her.

Maya quivered, but didn't move away. She stood motionless, mouth agape. Alex's finger darted in, out, and over her lips. The warm metallic taste of blood in her mouth. The pain in her hand faded, but sharp red dots remained. The tingle of yearning persisted, too, even as her heart raced in panic. The movement in her hips against Alex deepened and pulsed.

Alex's fingers quickened. Maya melted into her palm, softening with each gentle push.

"I like everything fresh." Alex whispered as she darted her tongue along the edge of Maya's ear. She smiled and picked up a blade, waving it over Maya's fingers. "You're so ripe and ready. So moist." Alex pulled her other hand from between Maya's legs.

"Don't," Maya said. Her voice pleaded, but she didn't know what she meant. *Don't take your hand away or don't hurt me? Did it matter?*

Maya broke into a cold sweat, but she couldn't fight the urge. She was disgusted, but soaked with sweat. Aroused beyond belief. The pain in her hand became a deeper ache. She leaned into Alex again, hungering for her touch.

Alex pointed the blade at Maya's reddened hand. "Put it on the counter." Not a question—a command.

Maya obeyed. The counter was cool beneath her palm. She stared into the simmering pot. Whatever Alex cooked obviously involved blood. *Her own blood.* And she wasn't finished.

Just one more ingredient.

Panic and aching lust flooded Maya with conflicting physical needs. *Run. Stay. Fuck.* No matter what the simmering concoction in the pot held—more than anything, she wanted Alex.

Confidence sparked in Alex's eyes. "You still want me, don't you?" Her lips curved, about to break into a smile.

Maya nodded and pushed her pelvis into Alex's hand again. Sweat poured down her face as she realized what she was about to do. Maya's consuming urges wove her into a fog. This want was like nothing she'd ever felt. *What if Alex was her one chance at love? Shouldn't she go for it? Say yes? Isn't that what real intimacy was about?*

Maya became liquid, warm and soft as melting chocolate. Sweat beaded all over her skin. She stared at Alex. Her eyes bounced from Alex's finger and the bloody notch to the edge of the gleaming blade, still glistening red.

Alive with her blood.

"If you are what you eat—" Alex paused, raising an eyebrow.

Maya shivered, bracing herself. There was only one answer.

"Do it."

Consummation of the Wasp
Christina Ladd

"The fig is the cuntiest fruit," she said, letting the tip of the knife dent the skin before slicing through it, a momentary tension I felt burst deep inside of me, in a place that had no name.

I was eighteen and I had never heard the word *cunt* out loud. I had never seen a fig, or kissed a girl, or met anyone like her. She had electric-gold hair and a smile as quick as a jab, beautiful in a terrible way. I didn't know how to be terrible. I wanted to learn from her.

She sliced toward the flesh of her thumb, the paring knife a sickle moon. The air was redolent with sickly sweetness, a thick scent that I pretended to like but that made me want to gag.

"Like fig bars?" I asked, because I hated silence.

"Oh, honey," she sighed. There was exactly as much contempt in her voice as in my mother's, and I wanted to prove both of them wrong. I took the piece she was offering and threw it into my mouth. And gagged.

She laughed at me. It wasn't kind, but shame felt like intimacy. Something shared. "Too sweet? Here," she said, and sprinkled something on it that I didn't see.

I hesitated. I still ate peanut butter and jelly for lunch. I still knew the name of every member of BTS. But here I was at a party—a *college* party—and someone was offering me an unknown substance, off-white granules melting into the juice of the fig.

She laughed again. "It's *salt*, honey. Salty, like me," she added, and tossed her hair in shining ripples. She was thrift store Old Hollywood, a ten-dollar Elizabeth Taylor decked out in cocktail carats.

She made herself a similar slice and touched our two pieces together, a makeshift toast. Then she sank her teeth into it and closed her eyes. Blissful. "Mmm."

I nibbled on my piece, too. She was so beautiful. I focused on that instead of the taste, which I still didn't like. The salt helped, though.

"You know how figs are made?" she asked, her mouth still full.

I'd studied biology two years ago and it was a bit hazy. "Pollination? Pollen goes from the stamen to the stigma because of wind or insects..."

"Most fruit, yeah. But with figs, the wasp doing the pollination crawls all the way inside the fig." She looked at me, challenging. Her eyes were as dark and deep as cellar doors. I wanted to know where she led.

One of the other people in the kitchen piped up as he went by. "Very Junji Ito."

I didn't know who that was. She laughed, though. "It was maaa-a-a-de for me!" I didn't get the reference so I took a sip of water, which didn't clear my mouth out at all. The salt-fig taste was thick on my teeth.

"But like I was saying," she continued, turning back to me and to the cutting board, "the wasp crawls in and dies there. Nice and cozy. And the fig digests her. Mostly. That crunch? That's the wasp. Mmm," she purred, and popped a chunk of fig into her mouth.

I wanted to gag.

"That's not true," said someone at the microwave, watching a plate of spanakopita go around. "Those are seeds."

"Spoilsport," she laughed.

I relaxed a little, stopped feeling like I had to keep my tongue pressed against all my teeth so that I didn't feel any little legs twitching in the gaps.

"It's only female wasps though, and female trees. Conservatives say nature isn't gay," she *tsked*. "They don't know their bible is based on older myths, ones about Inanna. One of her other names was the Goddess of the Fig. She had a bullshit husband, and a *sister* and a *handmaid*." She put quotations around the words with her hands. Her nails were very short but her fingers were very long. Big enough to span an octave on the piano. Big enough to fit all the way into my mouth, to stroke the bud of my uvula with a little *come here* motion.

I didn't know why I wanted that. The nameless place inside me felt full and empty at the same time.

"Inanna wanted to go down to the underworld to defeat her sister. *Go down*, like we don't know what that means. Only her *sister* defeated her, and she stayed. She stayed so long that the world above started to die. Her shitty husband didn't do much, but her *handmaid* went to the gates of death and didn't let up until Inanna came back to her. All the old scholars say it's about springtime, or mourning rituals, or the proper place of servants. But really, I think the moral is simpler," she said, and grinned at me. "Lesbians get the job done."

I buzzed inside that nameless place, glittering wings beginning to stir.

I didn't know what to do with my feelings, though, or where to put them. I was in a part of town I'd never been to before, in an apartment I'd never be able to recognize in daylight. The only other person I knew at this party was Jo, who had graduated this year. She was off making out with her girlfriend, who was a year older than her and who had invited us. I was just a tag-along. What did I know about old goddesses? What did I know about the Queer Student Union? I still had another year before college. I only knew I was gay by process of elimination.

She finished plating the figs, the radiating design like some kind of incantation I couldn't interpret. When she brushed past me to bring it into the other room, I felt the heat of her fingers on my hips long after she had gone.

Wanting to clear my head and *not* wanting to clear it, I went for the drinks table. I'd never drunk anything but Rolling Rock, but I liked the way it made the world crinkle at the edges, a cellophane feeling that wasn't even close to losing control. It just made the light bend a little different. I only wanted to be a *little* different. The right kind of different. I knew there were wrong ways, even here. Especially here.

But the guy beside me, pretty enough to be a pop star in his leather pants and pearl choker, shook his head when I asked for beer. "Only the good stuff," he said, and gave me the glass he'd been preparing for himself. It was mouthwash blue. I gulped it down and choked, expecting mint but finding orange. Shame and alcohol were twin burning sensations as I cast around for a towel, or maybe just a hole so I could crawl inside and die.

Someone patted me on the back, lingeringly. *Her.* She was laughing. "So much for that shirt," she said, fingering my collar lightly, brushing my clavicle like an accident. "C'mon."

I expected her to lead me to the bathroom, but she took me to a bedroom instead. *Her* bedroom. College students had their own rooms. They didn't have to share with their younger sisters; they didn't have to hide things and pretend.

She grabbed a t-shirt and handed it to me behind her back. "I won't look," she said, inspecting her overflowing closet instead. There was more black than I would have expected, more lace eating the light than rainbows throwing it back. The party noise was muted in here, the brightness dimmed.

She waited a respectable amount of time, humming to herself before turning around.

I hadn't put the shirt on.

It answered the question I knew she had been asking. And I was embarrassed by my cotton bra, polka-dotted and unpadded; I was embarrassed by the stubborn fat on my belly despite the crunches I did; I was embarrassed by the freckles on my chest like crumbs I'd forgotten to brush off. But she was grinning at me, and from behind a partial curtain of my hair I smiled back.

She walked toward me and I felt the room tilt. *Had* there been something on the figs? I felt dizzy, like I was walking up against the edge of a long drop, but also like I was the edge itself. I didn't have time to try to understand it. She was kissing me. Her lips stung mine with salt, and her fingers went creeping down my spine in stippling bursts.

My nameless place was filled with wings and crawling. No—all of me was. Every inch of my skin was

49

swarming, itching to be touched. Her hands weren't nearly enough.

She pushed me onto the bed as I fought with her dress, her bra. Eventually she laughed at me and undid it herself.

Wow. I understood those wasps. I would have crawled between her breasts and died there, happily.

"Everybody thinks the forbidden fruit in the garden of Eden was an apple," she said, crawling toward me, looming over me. "But it was a fig. Which just goes to show you..." she breathed, tantalizing me with the end of the sentence and the barest press of her lips, "...pussy makes you a god."

She began to kiss her way down my throat and I let my eyes flutter closed. Behind my lashes, there were more colors than I had ever been able to see—ultraviolet impressions bursting open like flowers.

She let me go on like that, drinking her in and unfurling under her like a slow spring, but I could feel her impatience from the start. I didn't know how to give her what she wanted, and she didn't tell me. I was so nervous I was trembling, my fingers grazing and alighting nearly in the same motion.

"C'mere," she said, but pushed me away, went for the button and zipper of my jeans. I wasn't the one she was talking to; I was just the person attached to what she wanted.

She eased me out of my pants and rolled my socks off, tickling my soles until I flinched. My smile felt etched on my face, as if it were put there by someone else. In my mind, I was in a papery underworld, grey and chambered.

I knew what I wanted—didn't I? I felt brittle, chitinous. Ready to crack open. I couldn't get my bearings.

"Who am I?" I asked her, hoping she would pause in teasing my legs apart and explain it all to me, the wild need and the hesitation both.

"Huh? You're..." She searched my face, but it wasn't until later—much later—that I let myself realize she didn't know my name.

"The goddess, the friend, or the sister? Which one?"

She laughed and bent down, and I licked my own lips like it was sympathetic magic. I tasted salt and sweetness, cloying, overwhelming. "Oh, honey," she murmured into me. "Pretty skinny little sting like you? You're the wasp. And I'm gonna eat you up." Her voice echoed through all the nameless places inside me, and the reverberations built and built, a stone dropped not into a river but into a furious hive.

The fruit of me split open, and the ghosts came pouring out. I dissolved into them—into *myself*—a hive of limbs and wings and glances out of fractal eyes. I was the paper shell. I was the brooding queen, and I was the thousand, thousand daughters.

She drew back from me, face slack with mirrored ecstasy, as if oblivion were contagious. One of me landed on her tongue, still fig-sweet. I crawled deeper, *deeper*. I could feel the soft flesh of her part for me and give way to the dark cave of her larynx. For a moment she hummed again, the sound of my little ghost nestling between the cords of her throat.

I crawled back into myself, the ghosts dormant beneath my skin. Except for one, who was inside her. Dissolving. Pollinating. Waiting to ripen. Waiting to burst.

Dex
Ali Seay

I met Dex at the seedy corner bar Dead Kenny's. I'd run away from Richard for what I was fairly certain would be the final time. Turned out it was.

Dex was holding court at the bar, a bright neon beer sign shining behind their head like a halo. They wore black trousers, high tops, a white tank top, and a black vest. Their hair was the color of cornsilk, hung over one stark blue eye and the other side shaved close to the skull.

My pulse quickened at the whole package. And at the Big Bad Wolf grin Dex gave me when they caught me staring.

"You lost, hon?"

I shook my head, trying to find my voice. Dex's long, thin arms were a mapwork of tattoos. Old school. All of them. Mermaids, skeletons, angels, and fish cavorted on their skin. I finally managed a soft, "No. I live nearby."

If by nearby you meant a thirty-minute walk in the drizzle down dark side streets.

"Ah, she lives nearby," Dex said. Faithful barroom acolytes murmured vague responses. "Beer?" Dex asked me.

"Sure."

"A pull for the lady," Dex said and the seats to their side suddenly became vacant as their attendees made room.

A girl could get used to this.

Four beers in, I was a bit googly-eyed and totally smitten.

"So, you left him?"

I could make out the vaguest pale halos of nipples beneath the white tank. The flash of a beautiful clavicle when Dex moved. The pink tongue nestled in the perfect mouth.

The sudden urge to grab Dex by the shoulders and plant a kiss on those lips made heat flood my cheeks.

Meanwhile, Dex's ankle bobbed vigorously atop their opposite knee. I noticed they never sat still. I noticed they hardly ever blinked.

"I hope so," I said. "Richard isn't always one to respect a girl's wishes."

"Hmph," Dex said.

I was again staring at the tender lower lip, a subtle, natural pale pink.

"Want to come home with me? I can keep you safe."

Dex was a lanky one—almost scrawny—but somehow, I believed them.

Not sure if it was the beer or the whole vibe they gave off, but there was no hesitation in my *yes*.

We walked. Dex lived about two blocks from the bar. The apartment was small, but cozy. Art and animal skulls lined the gray walls. The lights were all dim. The furniture—all shabby, but comfortable.

"Been here long?" I asked, just to have something to say.

Dex didn't say a word. They brushed their lips against mine. An electricity coursed through me. It was the sensation of both safety and power simultaneously, and that surge went straight to my sex. Their strong hands traced my body. I was curvy to Dex's straight, short to their tall, dark hair to their blond.

When they flipped up my skirt and hooked fingertips in my panties, I said nothing. When those panties hit the floor, I continued saying nothing. My tongue was too busy stroking over their tongue, and every stroke of their hands made me shiver.

A rash of goosebumps dotted my thighs and my nipples turned to little stones beneath my sweater.

Dex slyly smiled. "Excited to see me?"

I laughed. I couldn't help it. My buzz was wearing off but that intensely good feeling, almost a high, kept going. It was Dex, I realized. Not booze.

Then all the thinking went away because long, nimble fingers—fingers that would be right at home on the keys of a piano—traced slow, mesmerizing circles around my nipples. My sweater somehow disappeared, and the strokes were replaced by licks, and then the licks were replaced by nibbles.

Dex's long, lean limbs tangled with mine and their mouth captured every sigh and cry as those fingers entered me—moved in me—stroked me right to the point of no return and then pushed me over.

The sun was coming up when I turned on my side to find Dex watching me. I blushed, feeling seen for the first time in too long to remember.

Their fingers brushed through my dark curls and pushed the hair out of my eyes. They stroked the bruises on my arms and hips. The bruises were a mixture of dark blue, purple, yellow, and green. All the shades of chronic abuse. Then Dex whispered, "So how do we kill Richard?"

I waited a beat to see when I'd freak out. What kind of fear would invade the mellow cloud of happiness?

It didn't happen. I smiled at them.

"I don't know," I said. "Any ideas?"

I fell asleep to them murmuring, "I'll figure it out."

* * *

It was about eleven when I smelled bacon. Bacon was a good way to get most people out of bed.

I found my clothes and pulled them on. I went into the bathroom, peed, and inspected my sleep-deprived puffy face. I decided against brushing my teeth with my finger. It would fuck up the taste of the bacon.

Dex looked too good for having only slept a few hours. Today's outfit consisted of pristine white painters' pants, an old oversized, over-washed plain white tee, a striped navy blue and white tie loosely looped around their neck, and boots. Their hair was sleep-tousled and perfect.

In the daylight I saw faint fawn-colored freckles on the very tops of their cheeks. My heart seized up for a moment. A mixture of sudden and intense affection—and a raging lust.

I cleared my throat. "Morning."

"Ah, the fair maiden."

Dex poured me a cup of coffee, handed it over, and nodded at the counter. "Sugar and cream are there."

"Thanks," I said. "That bacon smells amazing."

Dex

Dex outlined my hip with a swish of their hand. There was a small squeeze right at the end. Almost proprietary. It turned my warmest places up to hot.

"If I give you bacon, will you finally tell me your name?"

I blinked. "I...told you."

"Really? When?"

I struggled to remember our conversation and felt a blush creep up my cheeks. "I guess I didn't."

I stuck out my hand and said, "I'm Dorothy. Dottie for short."

"Dorothy? Follow the dirty city road...to Dead Kenny's?"

"My mother was a fan. But I'd never been inside Dead Kenny's."

"Why last night?"

I doctored my coffee and then said, "Trying to get away from Richard. Fast. He had our car. Actually, he has his car. I don't have a car. Or a place to stay. Or many friends. I moved here from Pennsylvania."

Dex put the bacon on a plate lined with paper towels to drain, then motioned to the table. We sat.

"So, what was DK's going to do for you?"

"Hide me. I just wanted to be off the street before he came looking."

A succinct nod from Dex. Their pale blond hair fell in their face.

"So back to my question, Dottie. How do we kill him?"

I choked on my coffee and dropped the piece of bacon I'd been lifting to my mouth. "I thought that was a joke."

Dex turned my forearm over in their hand. A purple bruise, a bluish one, one that was a bit green, one that was an ugly yellow. Most shaped like big fingerprints.

Because they were.

"Is *this* a joke?" They asked, eyeing my rainbow of marks.

"No."

"Neither is what I said. People like that...they need to be stopped."

"I can't kill him."

Dex snagged a piece of bacon and ate it up in three bites. "I can."

"Why?"

"Why not?"

"You could go to jail."

Dex snorted. "Never. No one will know I did it. No one will look for me."

No one will look for me...

I tried humor. "And why is that?"

Dex shrugged. "Think of me as a guardian angel."

"A killer angel?"

They winked. "Have you ever read the Bible? Angels are heaven's warriors. Brutal."

"Brutal," I echoed.

* * *

I figured that if Dex was that brave, they could go with me to get some of my stuff. We'd parked a few streets over and walked to the house through the woods to avoid being seen.

I hadn't figured out where I was going or what I was going to do, but I did know that I wasn't going back to Richard.

For the first time ever, that option was off the table.

Maybe Dex's slightly insane bravado was contagious.

The house was quiet when we entered.

Tabitha made a beeline for Dex, appearing from the darkness of the curtained living room.

"Who is this?" Dex asked, scooping up the cat.

"Tabitha. But she stays," I sighed.

"Why?"

"Because she's his."

Dex looked down at the cat and said, "Do you belong to anyone but yourself, pretty girl?"

The cat seemed to answer and Dex nodded. "That's what I thought. She's coming with us."

I blinked.

"Do you think that someone who could do that to the woman he claims to love would necessarily be kind to an animal?"

I blinked again, then nodded slowly, understanding. "She comes with us."

Both Dex and Tabitha looked satisfied with this answer.

I was shoving underwear into a duffle bag when I heard the front door open and his keys drop into the aluminum bowl by the door.

He was supposed to be at work. It was a meeting day, no less. Richard liked to have one day a week where everything sucked. It made the rest of the week better, he said. So, he scheduled as many meetings as possible in that single day.

He was usually gone late into the evening.

My body froze before trying to go in every direction at once. It was a full-on panic, and I was scared.

Where was Dex? What would he do to me? To them? He walked into the bedroom with an amused smile. Richard was a big man, standing 6'3" and muscular. He was getting a bit of a belly on him, but his hands were still huge, his body still fast, and his ire still nearly instantaneous.

"I knew you'd come to get your shit. I knew you'd count on me being out. I know you, baby."

Baby.

Baby was never good. Baby was the endearment that came with a quick uppercut to the jaw, a slap across the face, and a punch in the gut. Baby was a fear word.

He undid his belt, and I couldn't figure where he was going with this. Fuck me? Beat me? Both?

I backpedaled, reaching behind me to find something—anything—I could use as a weapon.

I found a box of tissues and my ear buds.

"Richard, we can figure this out—"

Blue eyes like gas flames. He was enjoying this. He shook his head. "Nothing to figure out. You want to leave me and I'm not letting that happen."

"Wouldn't you be happier without all this turmoil?" I backed up, hit the bed with the back of my thighs, and then went down on my ass.

He crowded me and looked down with his predatory leer.

Dex

My fear spiked, followed swiftly by anger. At myself. How was I here? How did this keep happening?

Logic told me that I was looking up at the problem, but conditioning told me it was me. All me. I was broken and I was at fault.

He whipped the belt out of the loops like a magic trick and I flinched at the sound.

Flinching. So much flinching over the past three years.

"You should turn over and take your punishment."

He pushed me back with one big, splayed hand.

From behind him came a silken voice. "Oh, is that how it works here?"

Dex's booted foot delivered a swift hard kick to the back of his knee. It folded up and dumped him onto me. A surprised look on his face at being the one to go down.

"Dex!" I wanted to tell them to run. I wanted to tell them to get out and save themselves and maybe Tabitha, but I didn't get that far.

"Take your punishment," Dex said.

Something made a meaty slick sound, but I couldn't see. I was pinned under Richard and his body jerked in astonishment and pain.

"Dottie, what did you do?" he asked.

I laughed—a high, hysterical laugh.

There was a shadow on the wall that drew up and fanned out. My dazed eyes saw large palm fronds...sweeping birds...wings?

Another jolt from behind and he howled. I could hardly breathe. Blood flecks were flying; they dotted the air like red snow falling in reverse. Richard's blood painted the sunny yellow walls with crimson tears.

61

I was suffocating. I pushed against his big chest, trying to escape, trying to see.

His face a mask of rage, he snarled, "Bitches!"

Then the weapon—the carving knife from our kitchen—appeared from behind, and punched. The blade efficiently and suddenly sliced into his jugular.

Blood rained down on me. A thick metallic baptism.

The mean light faded from his eyes and his weight settled on me fully. My lungs, paralyzed by his outside force, refused to inflate.

I kicked my legs. Frantic.

Then he was rolling to the side and sliding to the floor. Dex stood in my view, their white outfit now tie-dyed with blood.

Their hair in their face, thin shoulders heaving with effort, eyes glowing.

I blinked, remembering the illusion of wings.

Angels.

Did Dex think they were an angel? *Did I*?

I laughed again. The humorless release shook my body like a quake. I grabbed the tie around Dex's neck and pulled them toward me.

I manhandled them once they were close and turned to see their back. A thin narrow back, the flare of shoulder blades. The intimation—the imagined presence—wings? Just my imagination, my fingers said.

No. No wings. Impossible.

Dex pulled back and looked at me. Blue eyes glowing with gorgeous insane light.

Insane.

Them?

Me?

Both?

"They'll think I did this," I said.

"I guess we should go then."

"Us?"

"Yes, together."

Dex's hands in my hair and lips on my lips. The dip of a tongue into my mouth. The squeeze of fingers against the roots of my hair. That subtle tug traveling swiftly like a brush fire through my body, pooling low between my thighs.

My breath came short again, but this time due to want and desire instead of fear and entrapment. A wet, honeyed need.

I kissed them, fingers traveling over the knobs on their back—real or imagined.

Inside my mind's eye, I saw the light die from Richard's eyes as Dex's fingers tickled up my inner thighs.

I gasped, surrounded by tousled bedding and scattered blood drops. My dead boyfriend on the floor and a hand that had just wielded a knife between my thighs.

When I came, I clutched Dex's hair so hard, I feared I'd ripped strands out.

The room smelled like blood and sex. Dex stared down at me.

"We should fly."

"Let me pack."

Dex shook their head. "Nope. If it's all still here, then they may not come after you. If you pack, it will look like you killed him and left."

Like I killed him and left.

Had I? Picked up an avenging angel at a bar and gotten him killed?

"Tabitha?"

Dex shook their head. "Sadly, no. But we're leaving the door open for her. She'll go to the neighbors."

"How do you know?"

I waited for the fear to come. It didn't. I waited for the guilt, and again felt nothing.

"A feeling."

"Am I crazy?"

"Maybe." Dex shrugged. "Does it matter?"

I shook my head. "I guess not."

In the end, I took the money in my wallet and the money from his secret stash. My mother's wedding ring. A book my first boyfriend had given me in high school. I dressed in my favorite clothes and took only those.

Dex put an arm around me, and I felt the brush of feathers against my jaw for a second, my eyes closed, face tilted toward the sun.

The house was surrounded by trees and big, chaotic swaths of overgrown land. The nearest neighbor was about a third of a mile down. No one saw us leave. We started through the woods back toward the car.

I stumbled over a tree root and fell to my hands and knees in the underbrush. It was wet and smelled like life and old blood.

Dex

Dex's hand came into view. I took it and looked up at them. Above their head, the gnarled remains of old vines and long-dead parasitic plants formed a halo above their chaotic mass of hair.

The freckles of blood on their cheeks and forehead accented the beatific look.

I stood, breathing in the scent of them. They smelled like the air after a heavy rain. "There's a bar down by the Gulf of Mexico that serves a killer margarita."

"Have you been?" I asked as we walked hand in hand.

"No."

"Then how do you know?" We reached the car and climbed in. Dex started the car.

"I read about it in a travel book. All the best things come from books. Thrillers, true crime, the Bible..."

A Change in Universal Flavor

Hailey Piper

The world spat Raine onto the sidewalk between a condom wrapper and patchwork wads of dried chewing gum, and she couldn't blame it. With a name like hers, she'd been getting spat out for all her nineteen years.

Past the curb, an engine growled.

"This is your last chance," Anderson said, lips curling beneath his auburn mustache. "Do something right for once in your life."

Past him, Stenner sat behind the steering wheel. Aviator shades dangled beneath his badge, but Raine had never seen him wear them. Cops only came for her at night, as if they sprang to spontaneous existence from the darkness the way people once thought mud birthed frogs and old meat spawned maggots.

The passenger side window slid shut, cutting Raine off from the inside of the black-and-white police cruiser. It gave a harsh chirp and then eased from the curb. Its stale aura must have been propping up her secrets. Now she felt the drug baggies loaded in her denim jacket's pocket, and the taped mic and wire sagged from her chest and bra.

Neither weight felt like doing something right, but she started up the sidewalk anyway, eyes peeled for a life to ruin.

Golden streetlights spread pale halos over the damp concrete. They reflected off leaf-choked puddles and glistened across the wet bricks of rundown apartment buildings that stuffed the street from here to the next intersection. The atmosphere hung thick with unseen cigarette smoke and wet dog odor.

And amid the grime and decay, Raine spotted an angel.

She was an unreal shade of chalk white. Luminous spines of light glared behind her head of milky curls, casting deep shadows down her bony brow, black eyes, and sullen expression. She wore a silvery garment, something between a tunic and a dress—Raine didn't know the name.

The angel parted dark lips. "You look like you might be pain itself." Her voice hummed with windchime fragility.

Raine jolted in place, first mistaking that last word for her name. "Pain?" she asked, and then patted her jacket. "I can ease any pain, if you need."

"Pain's transcendence is too great for a single soul," the angel said, and her eyes glanced skyward. "The scale is beyond imagination. There is a throne at the center of the universe. This was not its original shape, but the fountain of will is corrupted, its power spreading in fingers to seize all things. Someday, this will change."

Raine's fingers left her jacket and scratched her scalp-short hair. This angel sounded high already, and Anderson couldn't arrest anyone for that. Someone would have to make a purchase first, and that was only part of his plan.

"If you're looking to hit your head on heaven's door, I got the stuff," Raine said. The pitch sounded flimsy, but she could count it as practice if this woman didn't buy.

"Pain is the doorway to light," the angel said. "That's why I've gathered the others."

Others? That might mean a party. Raine could dump all these baggies in one night, the unfamiliar drugs passing hand to hand until she emptied her jacket.

"May I gather you?" the angel asked. Her breath chilled Raine's face.

"Sure, why the hell not?" Raine stuffed both hands in her pockets. "Let's bring some of that transcendence. Got a name?"

Streetlights glimmered in the angel's eyes. "They call me Angel." No surprise there.

Raine said her name, and then added: "Like the stuff from the sky." Another limp line.

But Angel's sullenness tweaked as if tugged by a subdermal hand. Not a smile exactly, but a pleased look drifted into her eyes.

A pretty look.

She turned and drifted up the street. Raine followed, and reminded herself not to let bodily wants play with her heart again. Such temptations had dragged her into this trouble in the first place. It began with the beers. She hadn't even liked them, but nineteen was underage no matter her ultimate preferences. Next came that time tagging the bus station ticket counter with a purple-painted message she hadn't cared about then and couldn't remember now.

Last came the almost-joyride, cut short when Anderson and Stenner picked her up for the third time. When they turned her into their dog.

And for what? Monica Albridge? Her family had the money and influence to snatch her from prison, and she didn't have thoughts to spare if she encouraged someone like Raine, with nothing, to bleed a little chaos into their small city.

So much mayhem and suffering, all for a straight girl. Raine needed to focus tonight, with her heart and sex drive on a leash.

Same as the cops now kept her soul.

At a chipped concrete stairway, Angel steered them into a seen-better-days apartment building and led them up a jumble of clanging steel steps. Their destiny awaited at the top in loudening chatter and music. Raine couldn't turn back now. She should follow Angel inside and warn everyone to steer clear of drugs and cops and Monica Albridge, to learn from Raine's mistakes.

Except helping them would mean hurting herself. No matter what became of anyone else, she was caught in a pig snare, more toothy and gnarled than any bear trap. She could either side with these strangers or grasp desperately for some kind of future.

There was really no choice at all.

A rust-colored door screeched open, hurting Raine's ears, and a guy in a plaid shirt opened his arms in welcome.

"The angel graces us," he said, eyelids drooping. Half-sarcastic, half-hammered.

"We may begin," Angel said. She nudged Plaid Guy out of her way without her lifting a finger. "I will need forty minutes of waiting."

Plaid Guy laughed. "Take the night."

Raine hurried behind Angel before the door slammed shut again. Its screech made her shoulders jerk, and her head bowed as if someone in the far past still shouted at her, still cared. When she lifted her eyes, Angel was gone.

"Forty minutos, chica," Plaid Guy said, sinking into the party's miasma.

Raine scanned the room for Angel. Her presence had put Raine's nerves at ease, and now they writhed to discomfort again in this crowd of unknowns. Partiers sat on bean bag chairs and sofas, or plunked down on the floor where they curled into each other. Beaded curtains draped various doorways, and band posters obscured one wall's splotchy paint job. A velvety red curtain hung half-open between the cluttered living room and kitchen. Hints of sweat and beer danced in the air.

No sign of Angel—fine. She had already done her part in leading Raine. Now came time to make sales, and to make sure they showed up on audio.

Supposedly Raine was part of a larger plan to—what, catch a local drug lord? Raise the crime rate? Anderson hadn't explained it well, or maybe Raine had been too terrified alone in that cold interrogation room to properly understand. She had only watched Anderson's eyes bore through her while Stenner stood to one side and played with his unworn shades.

But she knew to find people, and here she was, scheming to convince these punks and nobodies to buy from her. Say what, *Hey, want some drugs*? Which tactic had talked that first illegal beer into her hands?

Monica Albridge. Doubtful Raine could wield such charm against any of these people.

But Angel's words might work. The guy at the door had been waiting for her, and everyone else might have come for the same reason. Raine slid toward a living room corner where a couple sat with their backs to either wall, both wearing leather jackets bulleted with steel.

"Pretty cool to transcend, yeah?" Raine asked.

"That's why we're here, hon," one of the women said. Her mascara had smeared, but whether from crying or rubbing at her face, Raine couldn't tell.

"To cry for miracles," said the other.

Raine opened her mouth to follow up, but their bold confidence threw her off. She found the same vocal wall at the next group she neared, and the next. Everyone's chipper attitude seemed fortressed against influence, at least until Angel's return, and their heedless enthusiasm repelled Raine at every approach. She had no idea how anyone could be so certain of the words pouring out of their mouths. These people didn't need drugs; they were high already. Raine was undercooked for this crowd.

"You alone?" asked someone with a sandpapery voice.

Raine turned to find a lanky man smiling at her. His eyes hinted at a growing pool of alcohol in his gut, one he could scarcely hold.

"I'm not into dudes," Raine said, her tone flat.

She tensed for resistance, but the lanky man nodded. "Cool, me neither," he said, and then staggered off in search of someone else to smile at.

Raine's mic must've picked that up. Anderson and Stenner would have wanted her to turn the lanky man's interest into a sale. Not like they could put themselves in her position. No one would trust them enough to chat, let alone buy their baggies of poison. They were probably busy with their own cop games—Anderson twirling his mustache while Stenner tied some shrieking woman to distant railroad tracks.

A Change in Universal Flavor

Raine's thoughts faded along with the crowd's ambient murmur. Her head turned almost in unison with theirs to face the velvety red curtain, now mostly shut against the kitchen light except one spot a few feet off the floor, where it cast a halo around Angel's head.

She rose on the pads of her feet, growing taller as lights dimmed down the living room. Her silvery garment sagged down her chest, froze in the air until the apartment sank into true silence, and then shed away from Angel's nakedness.

Raine's chest tightened, nerves tugging at their leash. She hadn't realized the white curls of Angel's hair fell across her small breasts and down to her waist. A similar pale nest encircled the gentle member between Angel's legs. Above that, Angel clutched a tremendous sword, its hilt spiking in all directions like a blazing sun of bronze.

A voice of chimes and melody shattered the silence. "Tell me you're my pain, and I will reach inside," Angel said.

Seconds passed before Plaid Guy flinched from the crowd on some unspoken cue. "I am your pain," he said.

Angel tilted her sword and spoke again of the throne at the center of the universe and its fountain. Raine listened closer this time, wondering if she'd stumbled into a slam poetry show—except no one else looked prepped to perform.

Only Angel's head glowed with heavenly light. Only her sword looked ready to cut a slit in the night.

"A broken light is a rainbow, wearing the light's death in many colors," Angel said. "Tell me."

"I am your pain," Plaid Guy said, and this time a small chorus joined him.

"None will commit this murder to flesh." Angel raised her sword overhead, baring her marble-white nakedness under the shadow of her blade. "But I wear a self-pain."

Every word thrummed in Raine's ears as if meant for her and no one else. Her heart pounded—fuck, her clit pounded—the pair beating together in a steady drumming thunder. She wanted to hear more. Or black out. Or explode. If Angel didn't keep going, Raine might break into the poem's deathly rainbow.

Angel shifted the sword until it ran a line across her face. "Tell me."

"I am your pain," the partiers said together.

"I am your pain," Raine echoed, and it was a heavier promise than anything she carried beneath her clothes.

Angel drew the blade close to her face, against the skin, until it pressed the flesh beneath her black eyes.

A sting lit Raine's face. She pawed at her cheeks, and her fingers drew back, painted with crimson raindrops. The sting lingered beneath her eyes, and she wondered if this was the agreed-upon pain.

She glanced around the room. The studded jacket couple both wept crimson. Same for Plaid Guy, the lanky man, and everyone Raine had tried speaking with—their cheeks ran red as if gently cut by Angel's sword.

"A broken light is a rainbow," Angel said again, and lowered her sword. "My thanks for letting me gather you."

Soft applause circled the living room as Raine wiped red streaks into denim sleeves. Her heart thrummed on, ready to pump blood through the wounds beneath her eyes, and then she wouldn't have to worry anymore about the great hungry night.

But first, she had to speak to Angel, desperate as if checking a mirror to be sure she still had a face. No one else stood by the curtain or seemed concerned if Angel had hurt herself, or how she'd hurt everyone else. Not a blemish ran beneath her eyes.

"When you talk about the throne," Raine said, sidling closer. "Is that where you want to go? Center of the universe?"

Angel's eyes lingered on her sword. "It will take much more pain."

"What then?" Raine wanted to understand, or at least convince Angel she understood. "This corrupted fountain—going to cure that?"

"Change it," Angel said.

"I get the scale now." Raine pantomimed stirring a spoon through liquid. "It's like Kool-Aid."

Angel at last glanced up from her sword. Her natural sullenness bent in confusion.

"The pitcher's full of water no matter what," Raine said. "But you choose your little powder packet. Is it cherry? Strawberry? Right now maybe it's watermelon-flavored, but you want it lime."

Angel blinked in silence, but she didn't disagree.

Raine aimed a finger at the sword. "Can I touch it?"

Angel weighed the sword back and forth in one hand, as if interrogating it for evil intent, and then placed it across Raine's arms.

A heavy weapon, yet somehow lighter than Raine's mic, wire, and baggies. Maybe the sword was purer. She avoided the blade, yet for some reason the sun-shaped hilt's glimmer seemed more dangerous. Sharp objects knew their power, but bronze sunshine might have aspirations to greater threats. Raine slid the sword back into Angel's grasp.

Two fingers crossed the back of Angel's hand. Her skin was cold silk. How could anyone feel that soft and sleek?

"Thank—" Raine began but cut herself off at glimpsing her reflection in Angel's gaze.

On the street, she'd thought the shadows cast by Angel's brow painted her eyes black. This close, with nothing to obscure them, Raine realized the irises matched the pupils, made distinct only by tiny white cracks of frozen lightning. She leaned closer as if she might fall into their darkness.

The kiss was an accident, lips grazing lips.

Raine jerked back and clenched her teeth, still tasting Angel's cool breath. Had she learned nothing from Monica's chaos? She would die by these impulses if she didn't smarten up, and fast.

But Angel's curious expression, so fresh and vulnerable, stopped Raine from regretting the moment entirely.

And she had never tasted anyone so sweet.

She forced herself back into the throng of partiers and had almost forgotten she wasn't alone with Angel. Now Raine stared at every face, a reminder these people were real. She caught them laughing, wiping blood off their cheeks with napkins or sleeves. The gathering never weakened across the passing minutes, the hour. They wouldn't drift away post-performance and spare themselves the chance of becoming Raine's victims. They instead clung with their friendly expressions and damn open hearts.

These weren't prey for a pig snare. Just people, full of quirks and unpleasantness and life.

The baggies in Raine's jacket swelled to boulders and buckled her knees. She asked where to find the bathroom and then stormed across maroon tiles to a rickety porcelain toilet, where she lifted her top and then froze. If she killed this chance, there wouldn't be another.

But if she kept the wire, it would root itself in her heart, and the pocket baggies would feed it. She couldn't guess what that would make her, but she wouldn't be Raine the next time she looked in the mirror.

There was really no choice at all.

Her fingers clawed the wire and tape off her bra and chest. She coiled it around the mic, and it dropped like a thin black worm into the toilet. The baggies plunked a raindrop rhythm beside it before Raine flushed everything down the pipes in a gurgling roar.

Tank top still rolled to her collarbone, she washed her hands and then scrubbed the tape's stickiness and regrets off her bra and skin.

Her relentless scream charged from deep inside. She could only clasp both hands across her mouth and let it beat breathy fists against her palms. Its force almost blocked out the party chatter, running water, and the bathroom door's opening-shutting creak. Her scream fizzled as she turned to see who had stepped inside.

A mane of curling white hair circled Angel's face. She wore a silvery robe, its weak-knotted sash dangling beneath the V of her chest.

Raine's fingers crawled across her cheeks and nose until they covered her eyes. She couldn't stop Angel from seeing her, but she could stop herself from seeing Angel, and any reflection in her black eyes.

Gentle fingers clutched one wrist and drew the hand from Raine's face. She let one eye flutter open to darkness, the other to light, and then stared into Angel's blinding glory before welling tears stewed the bathroom into hazy maroon and white.

Angel first wiped tap water from Raine's chest, and then tears and dried blood from Raine's cheeks. Raine quivered harder each time Angel's thumb slid under an eye. She would collapse any moment.

"Raine," Angel said. "It was too much pain."

"No," Raine said, voice cracking, but she didn't know how to explain.

Angel's sullenness deepened. "Sometimes I believe the light is whole, and we are broken in ways too vast for pain."

Raine shook her head, but was there a right answer? A choice? She didn't know.

"But I also believe together, we can find a change." Angel spread her arms to either side. "May I gather you?"

Raine half-stepped, half-fell into Angel's chest, and then her body lifted from the mess of tiles. Letting herself go was easier than speaking. The world melted around her eyes, bathroom light giving way to a dark ginger-scented room of Christmas light-circled windows and a row of lava lamps.

And a bed, where Angel laid Raine. Her fingers danced across Raine's body as she settled onto the sheets, into them, and helped Raine undress. She brought a welcome angelic touch.

Except a thorn pierced Raine's heart, the cop wire's emotional parting gift. She needed to shake it out before Angel pricked her finger.

"Wait," Raine said, tears crystalizing again. "I have to tell you—I didn't come here for you. I came to do something bad."

Angel leaned across Raine, one hand hovering over her chest. "But all this pain you take." Dark lips whispered music in Raine's ears. "Are you here for me now? Are you the throne's finger, or my pain? Tell me."

Raine quivered with familiar words. "I am your pain."

And Angel reached inside her. They grasped at each other as Angel's robe spread open in a pair of protective wings, and tender fingers explored damp secrets. Muscles corded down their bodies. A new, different scream bullied its way up Raine's throat, and she had to bite into Angel's shoulder to keep it from thundering out.

The same sense of teeth sank into Raine's flesh, too. Not an angel bite—her face searched Raine's neck, finding unique un-kissed places and kissing them for the first time. Every returned touch slid cool brilliance across Raine's body. Each place where Raine kissed the sweet taste of Angel, she felt tasted. Everywhere Raine's throbbing muscles crushed against Angel, Raine felt likewise crushed, as if Angel were a mirror of sensations. Deeper than under-eye slits and teeth, pain and pleasure fought a war across blurring territories.

Or maybe this was pain alone in its truest form, a knowledge that beyond tonight, this kindness Raine gave and received might be the last she would ever feel, and she wouldn't know what to do with all the horrid emptiness to come.

They slowed, and then Raine curled into the circle of Angel's embrace and listened to her breath ease toward sleep.

Raine wished to sleep too, but her thoughts ran wild. This moment was finite, no matter what Angel said about the universe. Raine needed to leave this bed, party, and apartment before she lured a fresh hell here.

She wouldn't be Monica Albridge. She would be better than all the Monicas in the world.

Anderson and Stenner would be waiting. They would be all scowls and teeth, ready to drag Raine into a harsher pig snare, one without next chances or hope.

But at least if she left now, it was her move in this game of choices and chances. Maybe she wouldn't want to see her face in the mirror, but she could look and pretend she saw herself in Angel.

Raine dressed again, kissed Angel's brow, and drifted from the bed.

The apartment melted into a sloping hollow, ready to spit Raine onto the sidewalk if she didn't hurry herself down the clanking steel stairs and out the door where she belonged. She couldn't blame it. Life had been spitting her out for nineteen years.

Damp air squeezed her skin as she traipsed the empty sidewalk. Streetlights flickered, frail against the darkness, but no one haunted the street. Maybe Raine still had a chance? She stuffed her hands into now-empty jacket pockets and started toward the far intersection.

A familiar chirp jumped through her nerves. She didn't have time to run.

A Change in Universal Flavor

The black-and-white police cruiser growled from the darkness between two wet-bricked buildings. It settled against the curb, its lights flashing red and blue in Raine's eyes. Long silhouettes climbed featureless from either door, only crystallizing into Anderson and Stenner when they stood side by side between Raine and the car.

"Thought we didn't watch where you went?" Anderson asked. "That we wouldn't wait for you to come out?"

"Did you think we didn't hear it?" Stenner asked. His dangling aviator shades rattled against his chest. "What you did."

Anderson's earthworm-pink lips curled in a wet sneer. "You really fucked up, kid."

"I know," Raine said. Defeat formed a wet lump in her throat.

Anderson yanked her against the cruiser and clapped steel cuffs around her wrists. His hands patted her down, checking for secrets he already knew she'd flushed down the drain. She wondered if tonight had really been part of some grander plan. Had it even been an official operation? Maybe she'd fallen into a common cop game, played on private cop time through cop imaginations in which Anderson's and Stenner's pig snare tied Raine a little tighter to life's railroad tracks. For the fun of it, nothing more.

They were Monicas with badges. Maybe worse.

"You do not look like pain," a fragile voice sang into the night.

Raine clenched her teeth and glanced over one shoulder. She hadn't heard a door open or footsteps near, but there stood Angel, as if she had descended from the

81

high apartment on invisible wings in silver robe and bare feet.

And holding her sun-hilted sword.

Anderson lifted from Raine's spine in a cloud of stale heat. She spun around to look as Stenner joined Anderson, their rigid shapes crowding the curb. Angel's dark gaze pierced between them toward Raine.

"She isn't yours," Angel said, her tone suited for sweetly explaining to a small child why they couldn't steal another kid's toy.

Anderson's holster gave a leathery click as he drew his black pistol. Stenner's did the same, as much a mirror to Anderson's movements as Stenner himself. They each aimed at Angel.

Raine surged from cruiser to curb. "Wait, wait, don't." Her wrists tugged at the cuffs behind her back. "I'll do anything."

Stenner crashed a hard elbow into Raine's sternum, knocking her against the cruiser. He aimed for Angel, the pistol trembling in his hands.

"Drop the weapon," Anderson said, almost growling.

"Drop it!" Stenner shouted, and his echo shot down the street. "Hands in the air!"

Angel remained a statue, the sword clutched against her lap. Coils of pale hair tumbled from her shoulder as she glanced back and forth.

"Don't hurt her!" Raine cried. "She doesn't know what's going on all the time, she's special, she's, she's—" The words she needed were strangers; she couldn't call them for help.

Anderson and Stenner couldn't hear, or didn't want to. Their faces squeezed tense, blood pounding too loudly in their ears to catch Raine's pleas as they watched the sunlight sword.

"You can't take her," Angel said, her tone forever soft. "She is my pain."

"We'll be your fucking pain in a second if you don't drop the weapon," Anderson snapped. "Now."

"Right now!" Stenner shouted, arms shaking.

Angel's black eyes drank the night. "You'll be my pain?" she asked, perplexed and awed. She eyed her sword, motionless beneath her waist, and then glanced from Raine to Anderson and Stenner. "So you are."

One bare foot slid from the sidewalk as Angel's leg stretched from her robe. The sword tilted across her body, flashing the cruiser's lights across its blade.

Muzzle flares cast fresh halos around Anderson's and Stenner's heads as gunshots exploded in Raine's ears. She had never stood this close to firing pistols, and she crouched down and hunched her shoulders around her ears too late to block out the first rounds. Her panicked shrieking joined the second rounds. The third rounds. Both cops poured bullets across concrete.

Angel became a statue again. Her eyes narrowed, almost in pleasure.

Wet hot drops sprayed Raine's face as red ringlets burst from Anderson's chest. Another storm struck her skin when Stenner mirrored the bloody eruption, and crimson geysers burst from both their necks. Anderson jostled backward, and his head whipped sideways against the police cruiser, flashing a dark chasm where something quick and hard had driven through his left eye. Stenner twisted in place, his guts opening in a bright fountain. His blood-flecked shades sprang from his chest, and the dark lenses shattered over the pavement in a tinkling glass hailstorm.

Both men fell to the ground. Anderson's leg quivered, but for once Stenner didn't take his lead, lying still between the sidewalk and the street.

Angel drifted partway behind Raine. Her arms jerked as the sword snapped the cuffs, and she could at last hide her face in her hands again. She'd never seen dead bodies, didn't want to. She would see darkness instead and hope no cops grew here to haunt her.

Tender fingers gripped Raine's wrist and guided her hand down. The freed eye fluttered open on Angel's bright sweetness.

"Open both eyes." Angel drew down Raine's other hand. "I want you to see."

"What?" Raine whispered, her voice frail after all the screaming. "See what?"

"Beyond the broken rainbow," Angel said. "A change in universal flavor."

She closed her fingers beneath Raine's jaw and guided her sight between dead Anderson and dead Stenner. Their growing blood puddles slid toward the gutter as if filling the street's trough. Neither cop would hunt Raine again.

Angel kissed the blood from Raine's cheeks, and her nose, and then her chin and brow and eyelids. Her dark tongue licked up the metallic taste, and maybe inside someone unique like her, she could make its flavor sweet.

"We should run," Raine whispered. "There'll be more of them, bad as these."

"As these?" Angel glanced down her sword as if asking it questions and then eased onto the curb, her feet planted in the pooling blood. "Then I will wait for those who commit murder to flesh."

"Angel—"

"You may go," Angel said. "You have led me to new pain, and a chance for the broken rainbow. My thanks for letting me gather you."

Raine flinched back. Tension slid from her skin; she'd been released from her burden as Angel's pain when so much more pain would soon arrive. Wasn't this easier? Couldn't she almost hear the coming sirens? Best to walk away, run if she could, let the night take her in and spit her out on some undiscovered future. Wasn't she used to that yet?

Raine clenched her teeth and dug her heels against the sidewalk. This wasn't fair. She deserved better than a world eager to spit her out. She deserved to be gathered if she wanted. Yes, she could run.

But a mirror couldn't act alone. One needed somebody to reflect. Raine could return to Angel's side and sit with her on the cold damp concrete. She could be that reflection. They could squeeze close, tuck their heads together, and watch past the sword's end for a roar of sirens and flashing lights to fill the far intersection. The cacophony would pound in Raine's ears, but she'd endure, and she wouldn't leave Angel's side. They would wait, sword ready. Maybe with enough pain, those lights could shatter like in Angel's poem and bring a murder in flesh—a death in many colors.

And maybe a change in flavor, this time the universe flowing sweet as an angel's kiss. All these things could happen, or none of them. For once, there was a choice.

Raine only had to make it.

We Have Made a Home Beyond Death

Tiffany Morris

Deep in the thistle-knit field, we've abandoned our stories in favor of life. Moving beyond the place where we were left to die, our blood catches and recatches on thorns that bite into our strange flesh as we make our way back into the field where we now live our unlife.

In the last few moments I remember, the forest was shivering, breathing green and thick with daylight. A car, it must have been a car—a monster of shrieking metal and vomiting exhaust that clipped us off our path and sent us down a ravine. Our bodies tumbled hard in watercolor blurs of clothes, limbs, and blood—landing broken and heaplike in moss and gnarled, tangled roots. I was flung from my bike at a high speed. Jagged boulders kissed my skin as I fell, scraped and bloodied, along the stones. Against my ribs there was a cracking sharp pain, and a twisted something that stabbed through my chest. Then red, then nothing but the blinking back awake into a new and dull daylight. Renee's head was split at the back, her blood an elegant scarf soaking through the back of her jacket. Our bikes must have become twisted metal sculptures, tossed in the tempest of gravity, and lost somewhere on our wayward path. Would we ever find them again? Would we even need to?

I awakened in the red, nothing, duller daylight sometime after we landed. We stood and walked out of our bodies that were shed like snakeskin on the forest floor. I looked and saw Renee standing beside her flesh—perfect in her ghostly glow—radiant and beautiful. And she saw me. Without a word, we crawled back into our bodies like coming inside from the cold and getting under blankets—a soft homecoming.

"We're so lost," I said as I stood. I felt nothing as my broken leg popped back into the joint. "I shouldn't be able to stand, should I?"

"I can walk," she said, stepping over to where I stood. Her smile was radiant and strange, a long scrape at the edge of her bruised mouth.

The grey light surged, then dimmed. The forest was unnaturally quiet.

"Let's look for somewhere to go." Renee turned her head, listening for the sounds that might help us navigate—a brook, a waterfall, or a certain type of bird.

"I don't remember where we were going in the first place." I tried to think, but the tumbled images were only of our falling and landing. "Do you remember?"

"I don't remember much," Renee said. "Just us falling. And who I am, who you are, that I love you."

There was no breeze to catch her dark hair. She reached her hand into mine and we walked into our strange oblivion together.

***

A hard, wet thump cracked against bone as my love bludgeoned the man in the skull.

"This one should do just fine," she said. The man gurgled blood, moaning from between shattered teeth.

"Hush," I grinned down at him. "This won't take long."

The man groaned louder. I wasn't sure if anyone could hear us.

"Hurry," I urged Renee. Being discovered would be worse than true nothingness. We would not be captured, we would not be made oddities—we would not be exorcised from this earth.

Another hard crack followed a wet thump. Unintelligible whimpering and moaning called out from his busted mouth.

"One more," I said. Renee swung the heavy hammer back down. The final, violent thud put an end to the man's whimpering as his body convulsed and twitched—and finally, went still.

"Should we look through his stuff?" she asked.

"You do it. I've got to get to work on him."

We had stumbled upon his tent in a clearing not too far from the house. He had been alone, with wood chopped, stacked, and ready to be set to fire. There was a large hiking pack, too. None of this was of use to us except the knives and axe, and—crucially—what he carries on him, for every man is a harvest of flesh.

A knowing was present in my hands as I prepared. I felt like I must have hunted in my previous life. The knives were surgeon-steady in my hands as I did the work of gutting. I knew that we must harvest as soon as death happened in order to use the skin—in order to eat the organs. We would also leave some for rot in order to feast again and stay in our flesh.

We make maggot bread so we, ourselves, will not be devoured. We are somewhere between ectoplasm and mouldering, fleshy beings wearing the promise of death like a wedding veil.

Steam rose from the body as blood poured out, his skin gleaming like fish scales in the light. The air must have been cool, though I hadn't noticed any frost stiffening the mud and leaves, the branches of trees crinkling and withering as they shed their fullness and beauty—skeletal and lovely like my love and me.

Renee slung the man's axe over her shoulder and beckoned to me to follow her home. I tossed his bones in the lake and followed her soundless footsteps.

***

We have made a home beyond death: a cottage at the edge of the woods, before the fields of no-place, an endless fog that returns you back to the forest. When we found it, delirium thrashed into silence—soft against the daylight that weaved through the trees, outside of time. We were Lazarus perfect in our becoming, springlike, bringing forth flower garlands twisted from our uncertain revenant hands. Renee loved to wear them as we wandered through the woods, finding our kin in mushrooms and lichen blooming on the things that die, the writhing beetle and snake wriggling through wood wet with rot.

Every day, Renee tended a fire that licked the gloom in our yard. I wandered outside of our home to feel night-time once again. Our small house is beyond the reach of time, obscured in fog, where the quick flame of foxes screeches their lament in blurred visions, ducking and bowing in the thickets. It is only ever the grey of rainy daylight there. I did not have a measure of time in this place, so I wandered in the dark and did not sleep. Time had passed since the camper died, that was true, though I had no way to know how much. My wife and I wasted and grew, waning flesh like the moon, bloating rot then blooming renewed.

Through the stretching shadows of the forest I walked, moving from the deep grisaille of grey on grey in my home, wandering further into the charcoal and blue and velvet black, relieved of the coarse dull nullity of our home beyond the field and thicket.

I was near the site of the camper's death when I saw a distant glow of flashlights dancing. Voices carried in the deep night, brushing over my cold dead flesh.

Moving closer, I saw three human silhouettes, one aiming a camera on another glowing brightly in its light.

"—sightings of strange phenomena in this area. Two years ago, Henri Boudreau disappeared while camping. GPS located his almost-dead cell phone in this area, buried in the mud. His remains were never found."

A man's voice glared at me in the dark.

"My EMF meter is catching something," a higher voice yelled. Excitement sharp as a gunshot cracked through the air.

Fuck. Fuck. I realized what this meant: more people would surely come here. People would wander and seek the poor man's bones.

People will always look for ghosts.

The three silhouettes scrambled together and exclaimed happily reading the meter.

"Strange phenomena have been reported here since before Boudreau's disappearance," the man continued into

91

the camera. "Among them are odd sounds, such as women screaming—"

Those are the foxes, you fool.

"—and shadowy apparitions of women appearing and disappearing into mist."

Hot rage and cold doom rose bilious in me. We were not ghosts. We refused to become ghosts and stayed stubbornly in this place, never to disappear. We were staying together no matter what.

These people had to leave and never come back.

"You guys," the high voice said, "you guys, the reading is spiking, it's super intense right now. Look at how the red bar keeps increasing, this graph—"

I tripped backwards to get away from them. As I ran, their voices faded into the growing dark.

***

Renee didn't panic when I told her what I'd seen, and it made me feel a little calmer, quieter, more still. Clouds of grey shifted around our feet as I stood next to her. She always made me feel safe—her warmth and strength and big body all a place of home. Her deep calm in everything was so different from my feeling of smallness, of nervousness.

"Don't worry," she said. She poked at a log in the fire that fell, a bright column collapsing, and crackled. "We can always use more bodies. Their flesh will keep us real."

"How many more of them will come?" I insisted. "If we kill them, I mean. More people will come, anyway, but if we kill them, the police will investigate. Villagers, wanderers, ghost hunters, all manner of people."

"I know, Meredith," she said. "It's okay. We'll just have to make this place safer."

"But I don't know how we'll do that." A pause. "Do you mean like if we fortify this place?"

"There are things you don't know about it here," she said. "There are things that live here that don't live anywhere else. Things that I speak to in their own language, the language of unliving and unreal things."

I considered this for a moment, staring into the dancing flames once again.

"Is that how you knew? That we needed the flesh, the bread?"

Renee nodded and pulled me close to her. I tried to ignore the worry that pulsated in my unliving chest, my unbeating heart, the threat of an unknowable eternity.

***

I did not wander again into the night and stayed in the house instead, staring at the patterns in the warped wooden ceiling beams. This was a fine small place to be, a solid place beyond weather and will and want. A promise that was not heaven but was, still, life beyond life. I heard, for the first time, the sound of my wife speaking to the creatures in the fog. They screeched a chorus like women screaming. Like foxes did, I knew, in the before time. These are beings of air that guard the boundaries of life and death, Renee explained, keeping pristine the places where the two meet.

"Why do they let us be here, then?" I asked, and she just shrugged.

"They needed new caretakers," she said. "People who will help keep humans away from the area. They saw us die and led us here."

I tried to remember the walk back but my memories are only of the fall—bruised and bleeding flesh on stone that hardened to meet us and claim us.

"What if it's a trap?" I asked her.

"That had occurred to me. And I was like well, what if it isn't?"

I chewed the bread of death and swallowed hard, not knowing a good answer.

It snowed when Renee left, the creatures leading her out into the woods. I had taught her the business of gutting, the ways to stretch skin and extract organs, and to pull flesh from bone. Renee's bootprints led through into the forest's edge, where I could hear the mix of guardian screams and human screams, flashbangs of fear electric in the dark, the desire to live from the doomed humans as palpable as pulp. I didn't know what the future held, but I knew that when my wife arrived dragging their flesh in ribbons behind her, that we would feast and she would be beautiful in the dim light casting blue grey on the snow, far from the prying praying preying eyes that watch the dark for people like us.

Sirena's Collection of Tarot Cards

Archita Mittra

I'm thinking about my ex as I affix a framed picture of the *Ten of Swords* card on the wall. Inside the image, a man lies face down on the sandy shore, stabbed by ten pointed swords. A fitting punishment for cheating on me with the baker's wife. I picture Alex's face, filled with sand, unable to breathe or scream as the swords dig into his organs.

Yeah, he definitely deserved it.

"That's a scary card."

Caught up in my thoughts, I didn't hear the wind chimes tinkle, heralding a new customer. I turn back sharply, ready to greet the stranger with my practiced smile.

"Ah, yes. It's a card of deep wounds and painful endings," I tell her. She's young, possibly in her late 20s, wearing a yellow, floral dress that immediately lifts my mood. "But I hope," I add nervously, gesturing her to sit, "you are here seeking better tidings?"

Despite running my witchy shop for almost three years now, I still get a little nervous when meeting strangers. Her eyes trail across the room, from the cloudy crystal ball on the table and the salt lining the window, to the shelf stuffed with different Oracle and Tarot decks and vials of herbs, and then to the section of the wall where I have framed a few Tarot cards. Apart from Alex's card, there's also the *Hermit*, the *Devil,* and the *Two of Swords*. Finally, she turns to me. She lets out a deep breath, inhaling the lavender incense that I lit earlier to invoke a calming atmosphere.

"This is the first time I'm doing something like this," she says hurriedly.

I give an understanding nod. I know her type: the intrepid first-timer who comes in, looking doubtful and scared, as though they can't quite believe that they've exhausted all other options, and are finally enlisting the aid of a psychic to get rid of an unruly tenant or to take revenge on a cheating spouse.

She goes on, "My friend Rita suggested I come here. She said you could help me."

Rita is one of my oldest clients. We know each other from high school, and she urged me to start my own business after I correctly predicted that her relationship with a senior would end in heartbreak, that she'd get into art school regardless, and that her father had been having an affair with the housemaid. We meet every other week for lunch, to discuss our love lives and exchange gossip.

"Yes, of course," I say, shuffling my deck. "But first, you must tell me your name."

Her name is Lorna; she's a waitress at a nearby diner and one day, she wants to make it big as a Hollywood actress. I'm mesmerized by the greenish-brown of her eyes, like a forest pool filled with secrets. She's worried about her future and finances, and so I pull up the *Sun* and the *Four of Coins* to assure her. All she needs is an optimistic attitude and a solid plan for her career, the cards advise.

"I want to win an Oscar someday," she announces, and I'm impressed by her ambition.

The hours pass, and we turn to other topics. She has recently come out of a messy break-up, and she's still bitter about it. I think about Alex and how much he hurt me, as I reach forward to squeeze her hand. Even though I'm a fortune teller by profession, I sometimes feel that my job is more about offering a shoulder for jilted women to cry on. I promise her that she will find her true love soon.

"What will she look like?" Lorna asks, with a playful twinkle in her eyes.

A card falls out of my hand, like an omen. I lift it up and reveal it to her. It is *Temperance*, reversed: an angelic lady stands by a stream, pouring water from one cup to another. It bothers me that the card is upside down, but before I can explain the significance, Lorna exclaims gleefully, "I think she looks a little like you, Sirena."

I'm startled at how lovely my name sounds on her tongue and at the flirtatious lilt in her voice. She leans forward, her pretty face cupped between her palms, and I decide quite firmly that I've mourned Alex long enough.

***

I usually don't date my clients.

Lorna is different, I remind myself when she moves into my guest room and accompanies me to all of Rita's parties. I'm calmer and happier when she is around, and I slowly begin to share my secrets with her: the art of tea-making and drawing sigils, a few basic hexes, quick spells to dispel the evil eye, how to cast runes, and the mysteries of the Tarot. I tell her that the future isn't set in stone, and that the cards show the outcomes based on the choices we're most likely to make.

Her knowledge of magic and witchcraft is sketchy, drawn from horror movies and best-selling fantasy novels, and I have to patiently explain that pop culture is rarely accurate.

"Can you perform an exorcism?" she asks me, as I recount to her a recent trip where I had to go out of town to investigate strange happenings at a country manor.

"Yes, though I try to avoid such cases. They're pretty dangerous."

It doesn't faze her. "Can I come and watch, the next time you do it?"

"No. Didn't I just say that those are really dangerous?"

In fact, if I have to perform a heavier spell that involves me casting a salt pentagram and rummaging through my mom's grimoires, I pick a night when Lorna is working extra shifts or staying out late. I feel fiercely protective of her, and I do not want to draw the attention of the spirits toward us.

***

Some nights, we cuddle on the sofa, picking out cards that we are drawn to and asking each other questions about the past. When I draw the *Six of Swords*, I explain to her how my mother and I fled the city to escape my abusive father. There's more I could tell her, but something holds me back. She nods and presses a slow kiss on my forehead. It feels so lovely, and a tear trickles down my cheek. She picks out the *Two of Coins* for herself, and I surmise that she's secretly struggling with different choices, juggling priorities, her mind in turmoil.

"How did that audition go?" I ask. Rita's college friends are putting together a short film and looking for actors.

"Tina said she'll call me back if I get the role."

Tina is the director, a petite woman with dark green hair, whose past project caused quite a stir in film festivals abroad. I do not particularly like her but she seems like she can help Lorna land a proper gig. I can draw a card right now to find out if she will get the role or not, but I don't want to.

It was one of the ground rules that we made when we started dating: never ask questions about the future that directly pertain to our lives. I made that mistake with Alex when I was so determined to chase my happily-ever-after that I fixated on every small thing, and I do not wish to repeat that with Lorna.

Even if Lorna insists.

"C'mon, can't you just ask the deck if it's a yes or a no?"

I shake my head. "We've talked about this before."

Lorna pouts like a petulant child. Laughing, I pull her close and kiss her.

Yet later that night, after she falls asleep, I cannot help myself. Even though I like to believe that we have control over our destinies, I sometimes feel that we are still pulled by invisible strings. *Or perhaps, it's a way of avoiding blame*, I think as I tiptoe to the next room and spread the deck on the kitchen table.

I think about Lorna and Tina, and draw a card. Then, as though afraid that she will wake up any minute and catch me in the act, I shut the door and slowly turn the card over.

The Seven of Cups.

I flinch as if struck by an invisible hand. The card carries the image of a person, staring at seven cups, filled with untold riches and promises. But the cups exist only in the imagination, to hint at delusions and wishful thinking. Perhaps the wine has indeed addled my brain, and I have chosen wrongly and accidentally pulled out the traditional card for deception and infidelity. I shuffle my deck again and pick out three cards this time.

The Fool. The Moon. The Tower.

I sigh. Perhaps, I just need to cleanse my cards of negative energies; after all, I do several readings in a day for all sorts of clients. I burn some sage, place the deck on the kitchen windowsill, next to my small herb garden, and for added measure, put a selenite crystal over it.

***

When Lorna gets the role as I knew she would, I pretend to be happy for her even though it fills me with a strange sense of unease. Still, I buy a bottle of cheap champagne and put up new fairy lights. We spend a romantic evening in my apartment, getting tipsy and waltzing to a Sinatra playlist. We order some Chinese takeaway, and between mouthfuls of chop suey, Lorna keeps telling me just how amazing and talented Tina is, and how she is so excited to be selected for the project.

"Is everything alright? Did you swallow a chilli?"

Lorna's large eyes stare at me, full of concern. I must've spaced out, again. "Yeah," I lie. "The food is a little spicy."

"Wait, let me get ice cream."

Perhaps, she has noticed my discomfort because when she returns a minute later with a gigantic tub of choco-chip ice cream, she changes the topic and asks me all about the customized candles I'd finished making for a client.

***

With Lorna's long shifts at the diner and shooting for Tina's film, I don't see much of my girlfriend for the next few weeks. By the time she returns home, it is pretty late and we are too tired to talk. Sometimes, she falls asleep after hastily making love or halfway through a black and white film, and I am left staring at the wall, wide awake and feeling more alone than ever.

Even though the bulk of my income comes from performing love spells, I'm personally not a big fan of them. Nevertheless, I gather her fingernails and locks of hair and do a few spells on the sly, desperate to rekindle what we once shared. I want to think that it's not really a spell if it's *real* between us. The few times we are close, I trace sigils on her skin and whisper how much I love her.

She tells me that she loves me too, drowsily, her fingers in my hair.

I predict that after the production wraps up, Lorna will be freer, but I am proven wrong. One of Tina's associates has seen the footage and is very impressed with Lorna's work and wants to book her for an upcoming web series about millennial relationships.

"Why can't you just be happy for me?" she cries after I decline an invitation to one of Tina's afterparties.

"I'm happy for you," I tell her, trying to keep my voice calm.

"You're always sulking!"

"No, I'm not," I reply, even though we both know that it isn't true. I'm not really in a good mood these days, and even some of my customers have complained that the talismans I made for them aren't working properly.

Lorna paces about the room. "Tell me, Sirena. Are you jealous?"

I laugh, a little too quickly. "Of you and Tina? That's ridiculous."

She crinkles her brows. "That's not what I meant." She looks at me, and then, understanding flashes across her eyes, and I feel suddenly afraid. "I thought that you were jealous or scared of my career or something." Scratching her neck, Lorna adds, "Like the fact that I am finally going to quit waiting on tables and work on proper projects and I may have to move out."

"And... are you going to move out?" I ask softly, not ready for the answer.

"I might, in the future. It all depends on how well the film does, really."

By "film" I know she means Tina's project. The fact that she is now avoiding her name in our home makes me feel even worse.

***

We don't sleep together on the couch anymore, and some nights, Lorna doesn't come back at all, although she is considerate enough to drop a text to let me know at whose place she is staying over. But she still does her share of groceries and dish-washing, and we occasionally talk pleasantly over breakfast. I tell her about the new spells I have designed, and my heart flutters when her eyes gleam with familiar wonder.

"Sirena, will you do a spell to make sure the opening night is a grand success?"

The moment the words leave her mouth, I can see that she immediately regrets it. But I'm not willing to let it go. "Or, I could jinx it and make it an epic failure," I say smugly, pouring coffee into her mug.

Lorna's face is aghast. "You would never!"

"I just might." I smile with an air of mysteriousness that I usually reserve for my richer clients if they try to intimidate me.

"Well, if you do anything to jeopardize Tina's and mine's and our entire team's hard work, I'll I'll—"

She fumbles with her words, and I relish it. Goading her, I say, "Yes, Lorna, what will you do?"

"I'll, I'll…break up with you."

The words slice me like a knife. I fight back the tears, determined to not show her my scars. "Save me the trouble," I say, carefully spreading more honey over my pancakes. "We're over."

I don't look up when she screams at me or when she wails, begging me to reconsider. It is only after the door clicks shut that I let my tears fall.

**

Lorna hasn't taken any of her things and so I presume that she will be coming back.

I cancel all appointments for the day, as I feverishly await her return. I write her an apology letter, tear it up, write a new one and throw it away. She won't pick up my calls so I leave voicemails until her phone's memory is full. I write a lengthy text, send it, and delete it after a few minutes.

In the evening, I go for a stroll in the neighborhood and get kebabs from her favorite Indian place. I clean the kitchen and light a few candles. The scent of woodsmoke and cinnamon fills the room. As dusk slowly deepens into night, I call her again and again.

Finally, at around 10 pm, I receive a curt text: *Busy. Talk tomorrow.*

I throw the phone away. It hits the floor, and the screen has a satisfying crack across it. The idea of spending another sleepless night just waiting to speak to her is intolerable to me.

***

Despite the chamomile tea, the lavender incense, and the pills, I cannot sleep. I toss and turn in my bed, thinking about the cards I drew that fateful night, some three months ago. Tina's face swims up before me, and I think I hear Lorna's laugh echo across the room.

Hating myself, I get up and fill a bowl with water and place it carefully on the windowsill, so that it reflects my face and the moon within it. I light a candle and begin chanting in a low voice. The water swirls and turns cloudy, like a pond full of algae.

I keep chanting, and a new vision unfolds before me: I am standing at a window, trying to peer into the room. I can see the dark green of Tina's hair, falling unbound over her shoulders, and the sound of Lorna's laughter fills the room. I see Tina's hands cup her cheeks and pull her close.

Bile rises to my throat. I cry out in disgust, and the bowl I am holding slips from my fingers and crashes into the floor, splintering into shards.

I start puking. I have seen enough.

***

I spend the rest of the night carefully drawing a pentagram that covers almost the entire floor of the guest room. I light candles at all five corners, as I utter a spell of my own making, a spell I used a few times in the past. Then, sitting inside the center of the magic circle, I take out a small rectangular piece of paper and draw eight long marks on it, and a wavy line to represent a piece of string. I crush a fingernail over the paper, imagining her greenish-brown eyes and her lilting laughter for the last time.

Sometime around dawn, I fall asleep. I dream that Lorna is a famous actress and I'm standing in line to take a selfie. I wake up to the sound of the doorbell loudly ringing.

"I'm coming! I'm coming!" I shout, as I get up and open the door.

It is Lorna in a long, red dress with her hair disheveled and her eyes red from crying. It is still quite early, and I hope no one has seen her enter. Before I can say anything, she flings her arms around me and hugs me tightly. For a moment it seems everything can turn out alright. We can forgive each other if we so choose. Then I remember Tina's hands cupping Lorna's cheeks and I steel myself.

I lead her to the guest room, careful to stay outside the pentagram myself. If she notices the still-burning candles, she doesn't say anything. Instead, she takes my arm, and confesses, "Tina's in love with me."

"I know," I reply grimly, edging away from her.

"I turned her down."

I pause in my tracks and look up. "Lorna—" I start.

"I spoke to her and we've decided to keep things strictly platonic between us. And once this project wraps up, she promised to keep a distance." Lorna still hasn't noticed anything amiss, and it fills me with a crippling sense of guilt. "I like you, Sirena" she says, looking at me, "I like what we have, and I don't want to lose that, ever."

"Lorna—" I intone, as the thin salt lines slowly begin to glow.

"I'm sorry, Sirena—"

But it is too late. The pentagram is glowing and I push her away from me.

"What are you doing?"

"I'm...I'm sorry, too," I sputter, as the world begins to spin out of my control. "Please forgive me." My voice fails me as I shut the door and turn the lock.

With my back against the door, I fall to my knees, horrified at what I've just done. It is too late to stop the spell and I sit in a petrified stupor as Lorna pounds against the door, screaming to be let out.

***

When the screams finally stop, I gingerly open the door. It is filled with smoke, but there is no trace of Lorna anymore. From the center of the floor, I pick up the thick rectangular piece of paper that carries an image of my former girlfriend in her red dress, blindfolded and tightly bound, surrounded by eight swords impaled to the ground.

I purse my lips as I stick the *Eight of Swords* card onto the wall, next to Alex's card, and below the *Hermit* where I have trapped my father in perpetual solitude. She doesn't deserve this, but what is done is done. The tricky thing about weaving spells and twisting fate into your own ends is that you end up bleeding too, stabbed by invisible swords.

"I loved you, too," I say. A chilly breeze blows in from the open window, rustling the picture. Perhaps she can still hear me, from her prison. I weep for a while, mourning everything I have lost, when the wind chimes tinkle again and I hear footsteps.

I wipe the tears off my face as I get up to greet my first customer of the day.

Beaded is the Water upon My Wing

G.E. Woods

My dearest darling,

Forgive me my massacres, I have not confessed since you left, nor did I believe in it when you first taught me to put palms together. There is but a narrow path to survival for one such as I, and it was all I had known. Until you.

I remember the first time I saw you. True, it was your ship I saw first, that fattened beast I sang for until it slew itself against the cliffs. Ships have changed throughout the eons. This one was much more efficient than the earliest rowed boats that stumbled upon our island and later the great masted ships sailing at the wind's mercy. Yours bore a grey hull of metal, which, while not as helpful as wood, still went into decorating the island.

The weather held that day. Unlike some of my sisters, I did not prefer the chaotic retrieval of my meals from a storm. Our song was enough to ensure our needs were met. We sang the ship to the north end of the island where boulders cut through the water, fang-like and ready to snap. The hull warped and curled. There were nine of us then. Eternal, we should have been. We alighted on the deck, folding our wings back, then one by one carried the ensorcelled sailors to land, our wings straining against the added weight. I did not see you that day, for you had jumped into the water before we appeared, unaware of what truly felled your steed.

The sailor skins, as usual, were tanned for furniture and blankets. A wintry sea grows sharp talons, and our human parts are more delicate in the cold. Bones make useful building materials. I still have my lovely crown of molars, though I wear it rarely. There is no one to dress for. And the meat, of course, we prepared in a buffet of styles.

How many weeks did you roam wasting on the island before I found you? You, who clawed your way out of a hungry sea and clung to living, vomiting up saltwater when you tried to drink from pools too close to the coast—you, who spent your days clenching an angry gut after eating raw fish? Acrid vomit crusted your lips that day. Your skin peeled and blistered everywhere. I know I should have carried you back to my home. There was always room for more meat stores. But witnessing your struggle became a throbbing ache in my chest. I wanted to honor it. So instead, I dabbed your lips with a wet cloth and led you to an inland stream. You rolled over the bank's edge, crashing into the water, letting it devour you. I worried you meant to die, but you broke the surface, water clutching your thin shift to your curves beneath.

We sat on the bank, my legs folded beneath me, wings fluffed, your eyes staring blankly into the craggy greenery. When I shared a dried strip of meat with you, you hesitantly took a bite, then messily chewed it, your lips smacking. You called it "jerky." You didn't know then what you ate, or for several months afterward as we began dancing around each other on the island.

My sisters thought you a pet. They warned me not to name you, but they allowed our time together all the same. Did I tell you yours was the first soft hand that ever reached for me? My kin might ruffle my feathers or help me preen, but weeks into our acquaintance, when you wove your fingers through my wings, your mouth made a ridiculous 'O' as you brushed against the joint between my wing and naked back. How red-faced you always were in the beginning when noticing my bared breasts peeking out from plumage—you, who covered your body with scratched arms and folded your hands primly in your lap.

Had you been delirious the whole time? So much so that you never believed my wings more than a well-plumed cape? As we grew familiar, you would absently run your fingers over my feathered parts and be soothed—even then, you were barely present in reality, and I missed all the signs. But I do not know what I could have done. I had never cared for one such as you before.

You gave me many gifts during those months—regret, the most painful. I did not know regret before you arrived, as it was not a concept I lived near to. In those final weeks, you often spoke of your many regrets, praying them ceaselessly to your god—and I learned, in a way, to feel your loss. There is one regret that hollows me most.

That is not what I wish to remember. Forgive me. But the days are empty of song now. My memories are all I have.

You will not read this. How could you? So I ask, was loving me your final act of insanity? When you finally gave in to desire, and began to nuzzle your face into my downy breast. Inhaled the powdered coating of my calamus. And later, lowered your naked body until your scraped knees met stone, your long apricot hair strangled with knots, and you parted the short umber feathers between my thighs with your sunburned fingers and chipped nails and first lapped your dry tongue along my cleft—was that your mouthed confession telling your god you accepted the punishment you believed he cast upon you? One night, in sobbing agony, you screamed at me, "Demon." I held you as you wept, your body shaking and writhing.

Under a blistering sun, you explained to me how we were in a place named Hell and how you learned about it in your youth from elders both fearful and angry. And your being here, with the ability to live out your self-proclaimed 'twisted desires,' was proof of judgment for your sins.

My love, if that was punishment, let me sin again and again against your mouth.

But I do not know your god. He is an infant to my kind. And as you marveled at the secret places within me, you were on a slow march toward madness, praying ever more fervently for your imagined need for absolution…

Under a starry expanse, you explained how there were others. Girls whom, as a child, you thought pretty. Playacting as each other's betrothed, chaste kisses moaning into more. A hard fall for a visiting professor your first year at university. She taught you to open yourself to the world and to her. In turn, you taught me the same, excavating my oldest caverns—holding all up to the light, even the most terrible and lonely. I did not know goodness before you. It, too, was unnecessary. Now it festers within me.

A roommate caught you. You had lived in women's housing. No one thought to question the esteemed female professor's visits. You were expelled. She was something called "fired." Your voice grew distant, uncertain, small as you spoke of it, and I wanted to reach out to you and draw you near so you might never forget the residence you held in your own body.

Beaded is the Water Upon My Wing

Your parents had shipped you to a strict aunt living on the other side of the world who would see to the rest of your education. We made our own education, did we not? We learned what a light flick of a tongue here or a brush of feathers there could elicit.

You wanted to know more about my world. My sisters laughed when I taught you to build furniture and sew hide. Somehow you both lived with the belief that you were dead and that you might yet be rescued. You vowed to need no one else when you were saved and to devote your days to prayer and living alone. You said a trade would help.

I did not worry so much about you leaving. Each day, my joy grew more riotous than the last. How could it end? Play overtook us frequently. I even flew you around the island, your arms spread for my talons to grip beneath them. Landing, your eyes were dancing flames. Perhaps Hell was never meant to be annihilation, you mused. I asked what it was instead. You smiled and said Freedom.

A week later, you ran from me, your hands scratching down your face, screams echoing behind.

I was always cautious about bringing you to see my kin. While my sisters allowed our dalliances, I worried they might grow jealous or hungry for something fresh. You had fattened up on meat and the sweet herbs I taught you to pick. We took to covering your body in clay to protect it from the sun. When we bathed together, after you happily examined the water beading on my feathers, you would lie on the grass before me, letting me coax you into guttural states of bliss. I knew, my hands running over your soft flesh and wet folds, if my sisters saw you then, they would tear you apart.

But one day, dressed in skins we shaped to fit you, I took you to my home. I showed you our caves where we slept when it rained, and the oddities we scavenged from centuries of ships. In the coolest, deepest cave, we kept our meat. You asked where it came from. There were only small mammals on the island, nothing with large skins to tan. It is from the sailors, I said. I had not told you before because I thought you might be sad.

You were not sad. You were sickened.

Every time I drew near you—on the beaches, near the stream, under the wind-smacked trees—you ran from me. You stopped eating the food I left for you. I landed quietly on a branch and watched as you grabbed up handfuls of herbs to stuff into your mouth, a viscous string of snot dripping from your chin. A week passed. I tried to understand what had gone wrong. I found you standing on the edge of a cliff, swaying as you watched a parade of clouds over a bland sea. In a barren voice, you turned and called me a monster, said I had made *you* into a monster, too. On top of everything we had done, all the times we had loved each other, this was proof that you deserved what happened to you. Proof of Hell.

On a moonless night, while my kin and I slept, they arrived by ship, having learned of myths and terror, and eager for a hunt. You often wandered the rocky shores in the dark. I asked why once, when you began sleeping past dawn. You said it was because, in your world, a woman does not get to walk alone at night. I had been alone in a world of perpetual darkness. Your fire inside me could not be quelled, and somehow, I had ruined us, destroying what little sense of humanity you thought you still carried.

My darling, you were never a monster. You *lived*. There is no shame in that.

Beaded is the Water Upon My Wing

The sound of the sailors slaughtering my kin reached you on the shore. A violet dawn turned us into shadow puppets on the cliff, like you sometimes played on the walls of the cave you took refuge in, and where we continued exploring each other's bodies when violent skies thrashed the island—me, mesmerized by a body so delicately naked. You, in turn, wondering at wings that might lift you away from all the dread you carried inside.

That night, our feathers drowned in pools of blood. My sisters sang into battle as best they could, but the sailors had taken to slitting our throats and plugging their ears. In the end, it was a lone man standing on the cliff and me. Bent at an awkward angle, I stumbled backward on my bloodied leg but could not gain lift with my injured wing. The man held out a jagged knife and bounced on his feet. Lightning flashes shattered his movements in stuttered motion. And there you came, climbing up the rocks, your hands calloused, your feet sure, your mind breaking across all the jagged rules your world had cut you against.

As he lunged for me, I only watched your face, rage twisting your mouth. I knew what you meant to do, and I was powerless—my hands limp, one wing hanging.

Your bodies went over the cliff, and the sea swallowed you without a sound.

In the days after, I sunk their ship and wandered the island looking for any trace of you. I never found the small, speeding boat they used to sneak into my home. Did you drown with the sailor, and the boat capsized? Are you dead? Do you live?

The ocean does not make offerings anymore, and ships do not pass, nor do I care to sing. For a time, I had

115

something greater. What is song anymore but empty notes that will never match what the sea has taken?

May this letter never find you, for being found means you have lived.

But not with me.

Do not return.

***

Date: 1962

I rowed as far from my sins as I could. From the island. From you.

A shipping boat dredged me out of the water. The sailors thought me a ragged mermaid, but you'll enjoy their disappointment upon realizing I was barely a woman—so wild I had become. They returned me home, where I was trussed up as fast as my parents could manage and sent to the first husband they could pay. "Unstable," they whispered when I neared.

For months, I thought you a terrible dream. Daily I went to confession after nights filled with feathers and eager mouths. The priests kept my confidence but warned me that this delirium was a vision of what my life would be if I kept to the path of loving the fairer sex. But I cannot forget your face. You haunt me as surely as your song haunts those you sing to their deaths. But it is how you were made. Day after day, I remember how crushed you were when I called you 'monster'. You gave me life, and I damned you for it.

After a year of a dour marriage, my husband came into money. I urged him to buy a ship. He sleeps beneath it in the harbor now.

My darling, sing for me.

Beaded is the Water Upon My Wing
I'm coming home.

The Blessing
Alex Luceli Jiménez

You have heard how Maria came to town. It was passed around as chisme often enough. Maria came to town the night Adora lost her doll. Actually what happened was the airport lost her doll when it lost her luggage the night Adora made the trip from New York back to her small central California hometown to attend her mother's funeral. She showed up at her dead mother's house shaking and sobbing and her aunts and cousins hugged her and tried to calm her down, tried to tell her that her mother was in a better place, and it wasn't until Adora had regained control of her breathing that she screamed out the name of her beloved doll: Maria. They were all in the living room huddled around Adora, who sat in her dead mother's armchair and trembled and clutched at her sides like she was about to break. They all heard the unlocked door open, and thought it was another cousin, or another aunt, or a neighbor coming to pay their respects. Nobody turned around to see the woman entering the living room—not until they heard that sing-songy voice speak, "Adora, I'm here."

When the huddled mass turned to look, there she was—blonde, beautiful, and wearing the same silk green dress Adora's doll had always worn, the same stark white gloves that covered up the left porcelain hand that Adora had broken and hot-glued back on. Like an ocean being parted, they all moved so the woman who looked so much like Adora's doll could fall at the weeping Adora's feet. She fell with grace, her long arms reaching up to wipe away Adora's tears. Adora stared at her in wonder, crying silently. She spoke the name again, "Maria?"

"It's me," said Maria, because it could only be Maria. "Don't cry anymore. I'm here."

***

Maria was the porcelain doll that Adora's father gave her when she was six and he was still six months away from putting a bullet in his head. You know that because everyone in town knew that. You saw her carrying that doll in her arms, too. She carried that doll in her arms until she turned thirteen, and after that she started keeping it in her backpack or tote bag, but everyone knew she had it with her even if they couldn't see it. Everyone was so used to it, they called Adora la güera and Maria la güerita with their matching blonde hair.

When Adora shut herself in her dead mother's house after the funeral and told everyone to leave her alone, everyone listened. Even if they thought it was a little odd how that Maria woman looked so much like that Maria doll, no one wanted to say anything. Lord knows cruel kids and their gossiping parents could've done leagues more harm than just pressuring Adora into hiding Maria away in her later years, but there was something about that doll that made their tongues quake and quiver before stopping altogether. Like she'd been cast with some kind of protective magic that made her and Adora untouchable, or maybe the doll had cast the magic herself. That's what they secretly believed, anyway, so they wouldn't have to think too hard about what it must have been like to grow up the way Adora did, with a father who committed suicide and an overworked, alcoholic mother who emerged to socialize exclusively on Sunday mornings when she and Adora and Maria sat down at the church pew and bowed their heads and pretended they were good and loyal Catholics. The only Catholic sensibility about Adora, anyway, was that she'd named Maria after the Virgin of Guadalupe candles her aunts would bring around because she'd always liked watching the flames flicker.

So no one except Samantha Cruz, who lived across the street from Adora, cared enough to call it what it was: Maria hadn't just come to town, she had come to life. Starting the night Maria came to life, Sam kept a watchful eye on the house from her bedroom window, which faced the street. So did Adora's bedroom window, but Adora's blinds were always shut. From her window, Sam watched Maria the one time she left the house to buy groceries from the corner store, watched her come back with an armful of paper bags and disappear right back into the house. Everyone in town had seen Adora and her doll, but with Sam it was different. She had been Adora's only friend for years, a consequence of their proximity and their shared age and the fact that Sam's mother felt bad for Adora and pressured Sam into playing with her when they were growing up. Sam had always thought Maria was creepy and when she asked Adora not to bring her doll when she came over, Adora listened. Sam was the only person for whom Adora would put away that damn doll. They were close in elementary and middle school, but more distant in high school. Everything between them came to a full stop when they were sixteen and Adora showed up on Sam's doorstep with a love confession poem in a white envelope, Maria in her arms when she said, "Sam, I want you to know that I love you as more than a friend and I wrote this poem for you."

And Sam, who could only look at Maria, shook her head and said, "I'm sorry, Adora, it's not that I'm straight but I just don't feel that way about you."

And she wouldn't accept the poem and they stopped talking after that but Sam still cared about Adora. How could she not when they'd known each other since they were infants? The truth is, Sam could see that something burned bright in Adora, something no one else in town wanted to see—don't lie and act like *you* saw it, too—because all they saw was that doll.

Sam looked at Adora's house and its closed blinds. The word *wrong* rang through her mind and she decided to do something.

***

Adora was in her childhood bed wearing the same clothes she'd been wearing at her mother's funeral when the doorbell rang. Her face was rigid with dry tears. She hadn't spoken to her mother since she left town at eighteen. Now her mother was dead and she had inherited her house. You know that, at least. It was passed around as chisme often enough.

But she wasn't alone. She had Maria, who was taking care of her. Maria, who opened the door so Adora wouldn't have to get up. Adora heard the door open and then the murmur of voices and then a familiar voice:

"What the hell do you mean I can't come in?"

And then, from that same voice:

"Adora? Adora, can you hear me?"

The Blessing

Adora sat up in bed, and listened to loud footsteps crash their way up the stairs. She was stepping outside of her bedroom door when she saw Sam step up the top step, eyes blown wide and her hands balled into fists.

"Sam?"

"Adora?" Sam came closer, her hands flexing now, like she wanted to touch Adora to make sure she was real. "Are you okay?"

Then came Maria behind Sam, eyes narrowed and arms crossed. She was still in that green silk dress, and still wearing those stark white gloves. The material wasn't so pristine after a week of life. She had dark stains on the dress and on the gloves; they weren't so stark white anymore.

"I told her not to come in," said Maria. "I told her you were sleeping."

"It's okay," said Adora. "What's going on, Sam?"

"I just wanted to make sure that you're okay. You haven't come out of the house in a week."

"I've been tired."

"So…" Sam was slumped now, like the fight in her was gone. "So you're fine?"

"Yes, Sam. I'm fine."

Sam looked at Maria behind her, warily, and then back at Adora.

"Still," she said, "if you're up for it, I'd like to take you to dinner tomorrow night. I know you've been going through a lot. We can catch up, like old times."

Adora looked at Maria, whose face betrayed nothing. "I don't know if I'm up for it."

"C'mon, Adora—"

"She said no," said Maria.

"I wasn't asking you," said Sam, arms crossed now in a mirror image of Maria's pose. She said this without looking at Maria, and again Adora looked at Maria and then at Sam. Sam kept going, "C'mon, Adora. It'll be like old times."

And Sam had always been the only person for whom Adora would leave Maria, so she closed her eyes and sighed and nodded.

"Okay," she said.

**

You know Sam took Adora to that fancy Italian restaurant downtown, the only nice place in town. It was passed around as chisme. They did catch up, but it wasn't like old times.

Sam asked, "So how have you been?"

And Adora said, "Well, my amá just died. So."

And Sam asked, "So how's New York?"

And Adora said, "Dirty. Loud."

Sam laughed, and said, "I guess I wouldn't know. You know I could never get out of this town. I'm still a checkout girl at the grocery store, but I'm taking night classes and I want to be a nurse."

That finally made Adora smile, and she said, "You always wanted to be a nurse."

"I'm living the dream," said Sam, and after that it wasn't awkward.

It was awkward again when dinner was over and they were walking to Sam's car and Adora suddenly reached over and grabbed Sam's hand, and both of them stopped in the middle of the parking lot. This was also passed around as chisme.

"Do you think," began Adora, "that you might ever feel differently?"

And Sam knew what Adora was talking about, but she still said, "What?"

"I told you I loved you when we were sixteen," said Adora. "What if I still do?"

And Sam knew she was going to break Adora's heart again, but she still said, "I'm sorry, Adora—"

Adora didn't let her finish. She dropped Sam's hand and said, "You pushed past Maria to get into my house. You asked me to have dinner."

"I care about you. That doesn't mean—it just didn't mean I love you, but I still care."

The car ride home was silent.

***

You can't have known most of this, but you definitely didn't know this—when Adora came home from dinner with Sam, Maria was sitting in her dead mother's armchair and all it took was one look for Maria to say, "Come here."

Then it was Adora's turn to fall at Maria's feet, in tears like the night Maria came to life. She sobbed in Maria's lap and Maria stroked her hair and whispered, "You deserve better."

Then Maria coaxed Adora to her feet, and they both stood, and whether it was Adora or Maria who kissed the other first, who could say.

Then they stumbled up the stairs and into Adora's bedroom, and before they fell into bed together, Maria opened the blinds.

"I want to see you in the moonlight," she told Adora, and Adora did not question this. And this was how Adora learned that underneath Maria's left glove, her pale hand was connected to her pale wrist with a jagged black line, slightly unaligned, just like when Maria was still a doll.

Who knows if anyone but Sam saw them through the window. Sam saw them, and she did not pass it around as chisme.

***

You may have heard about how the day after Sam took Adora to dinner, Sam crossed the street at 8 a.m. and started pounding on Adora's front door until Maria opened it, frowning.

"Yes?"

"I need to see Adora."

"She's sleeping."

"I need to see her."

Then she started pushing past Maria again, like she had before, but this time Maria shoved her once—hard—until Sam was standing on the welcome mat again with wide eyes and trembling hands. The mailman saw this, and it was passed around as chisme.

"Leave us alone or you'll be sorry," Maria told Sam. Then she shut and locked the door.

***

Something else you couldn't have known: Adora woke up shortly after Maria shoved Sam, blinking her eyes open to see Maria sitting on the foot of her bed. Her back was turned to her but there was something in the curve of her back that alerted Adora. Maria never hunched over like that.

"Maria?"

"That girl Samantha came by."

"Sam came by?" Adora sat up, interest piqued. "What'd she say?"

"She's worrying me."

"What do you mean?"

Now Maria stood, and came over so that she was standing over Adora, a solemn look on her face.

"She can be dangerous," said Maria, "if we let her be."

"I don't understand," said Adora.

"She knows who I am. What I am. I can tell."

"You're just Maria. What's so bad about that?"

"Not everyone can see that. Not everyone can see that I'm a blessing."

"But you are." Then Adora reached up and grasped at Maria's face, and Maria put her gloved hand over one of Adora's.

That's when a rock hit Adora's window, and it made Adora jump, but Maria didn't flinch.

"Adora!" Sam's voice was muffled, and another rock hit the window. This, too, was passed around as chisme. The neighbors watched and whispered and someone even stuck their head out their front door and told Sam to shut up. "Adora!"

"Do you see what I mean?" Maria looked down at Adora, and another rock hit the window. "Do you see the lengths to which she will go?"

Adora shook her head, and stood to go over to her window, which she opened just as Sam was about to throw another rock.

"Sam, what's going on?"

"Is she keeping you in there, Adora?"

Adora shook her head, and felt Maria come up behind her.

"I'm fine, Sam," she called out, her voice nearly carried away in the breezy morning. "Go home."

"I'm worried about you, Adora."

You know she said that. It was passed around as chisme.

"Go home, Sam."

Then Adora shut the window. That, too, was passed around as chisme.

But Sam did not go home. Sam sat with her legs crossed on Adora's front lawn, covered in dead grass, and Adora watched her from her bedroom window with Maria by her side and sighed.

"I should go talk to her," said Adora, and Maria shook her head.

"Why should you give her what she wants?" That, left unsaid, was clear enough—when had Sam ever given Adora what she wanted?

Adora said nothing for a long time. Finally, she turned and said, "I'm going to go talk to her."

She made it all the way down to the living room before Maria's hand touched her shoulder, and halted her.

"Wait," said Maria. Then she walked into the kitchen, and came back with a butcher knife that Adora's mother had used only once. She handed it to Adora, and Adora took it instinctively because it was Maria who was giving it to her.

"What's this for?"

"Invite her in," said Maria, "and get rid of her."

Adora did not have to ask what Maria meant by that. She had spent a lifetime imagining what Maria might say to her if she came to life. She shook her head, and handed the knife back.

"I can't do that to her," she told Maria. She turned, and walked to the front door, and opened it. When Sam saw her, she scrambled to stand up and sprinted over.

"Adora," said Sam, and all the questions she had were contained in that single utterance.

"I'm fine, Sam," said Adora. "I don't know why you're so worried."

"It's just that I saw…" Sam shook her head. Her face was red. "Never mind. It doesn't matter what I saw. It just matters that you're okay."

"Why don't you come in?"

Sam stepped into the entryway, and Adora closed the door behind her. They stayed there in that entryway, with Adora's back turned to the door and Sam's back turned to the entrance that connected the entryway to the living room.

"What's the matter, Sam? Why are you so worried?"

"I don't know how you can stand it," Sam said. "Being in here all alone with that—that thing. That doll."

"She's not a doll anymore, though, is she?"

"I guess not. But still. It's insanity, that's what it is."

"You shouldn't talk so much about things you can't possibly understand."

That's when Maria appeared, knife in hand. Adora's brown eyes met Maria's blue ones, and she knew what Maria meant to do. She had spent a lifetime imagining what Maria might do if she came to life.

"Sam," said Adora, slowly, "I need you to leave."

"Already? But we just—"

Adora reached behind herself, and flung the front door open, and Maria retreated into the living room unseen by Sam.

"Now," said Adora, and Sam saw it then: something bright still burned in Adora, and it was asking her, with everything she had, to just listen. Before she left, she looked over her shoulder almost thoughtlessly—too late for it to be meaningful. Adora watched her until she was inside her own house, and then she closed the door.

***

Sam did not retreat further into her own house. She stayed there in her own entryway for a long time, back pressed against the door. She turned it around over and over in her mind—the way Adora had commanded that she leave. So much authority in her lanky frame that Sam had never seen before. The word *wrong* rang through her mind, like it had been ringing since that doll came to life. Finally she opened her front door again, and stood there on her porch steps staring at Adora's house with its shut door, and that's when she heard the scream. A top-of-your-lungs scream, with all the authority that Adora had possessed when she told Sam to leave. You know about this scream—

it was passed around as chisme. Sam took off running towards Adora's house. You know how fast she ran—it was passed around as chisme. Adora hadn't locked the door and Sam opened it and let herself in. You know she let herself in—it was passed around as chisme.

What you cannot know is this: what Sam saw when she stepped into Adora's living room, what she saw on the living room floor. What you do know is this—that Sam let out the second scream heard by that neighborhood, and it was even louder than the first.

***

You have heard that Adora left town. Sam heard the scream, ran into the house, and then she screamed, too. But no one knows why she screamed, or why there was a first scream in the first place. By the time Sam stepped foot into Adora's house, Adora was already gone. Sam stumbled out of an empty house and into the middle of the street with two porcelain dolls in her arms. You know this; it was passed around as chisme. Sam's mom, along with troves of nosy neighbors—don't lie and say you weren't among them—joined Sam out on the street until she was surrounded and shaking.

"What happened?" asked a chorus of voices. "What happened, what happened?"

And Sam clutched the dolls closer but everyone could see: la güerita they'd seen all their lives, in the arms of la güera, and one that looked just like la güera. One blonde doll wearing a dirty green silk dress and dirty white gloves, and one blonde doll wearing black lounge pants and a gray cardigan. Strange, you thought—because that's what everyone thought—but did anyone ever look beyond that? They just heard that Adora was gone again. She'd found a way out again. A way out, again, after all she had been through? What a blessing.

She Lingers Like Smoke
Kat Siddle

I arrived with the smoke. As I drove, the sunlight changed from copper to pink, then faded completely. By the time I reached my mom's house, the sky was the colour of sour milk and the sun was a fluorescent circle, just a little bigger than the moon.

"Hi sweetheart," my mom said when she answered the door. "Bad luck with all this." She nodded at the sky. "Come inside quickly, don't let it in."

"I feel like I just smoked half a pack of cigarettes," I said, leaning in for a quick hug.

"We'll have to stay inside the whole time. They say it won't lift for a week at least. I'm so sorry about the timing." She looked crushed, like she was personally responsible for the winds that had pushed the smoke of a California mega-fire into her home, 800 miles away.

"It's fine. We'll find stuff to do. Maybe I can fix some things around the house."

She frowned. She never really liked it when her only daughter played handyman, as she put it. But she didn't say no, either. She made tea and I drank it fast, trying to wash the taste of burning forest out of the back of my throat. We decided we'd clean out the basement. Not as fun as fixing something, but I took a certain satisfaction from the plan. Mom had been complaining about the clutter down there for years.

We started after dinner. Mom sat on the floor and sorted things into piles while I ferried boxes of books and Betamax tapes out of the storage room.

That's when I started seeing the woman. I walked into the storage room and she walked out, vanishing into the wall like she was stepping into an elevator. Her back was to me, but I caught the movement of her skirt, the swing of her hair.

I took a step back and blinked hard, trying to figure out what I'd just seen.

"You okay?" my mom asked.

"Dust in my eyes," I said, rubbing my face. "Making me see things."

My mom sighed loudly enough to make me turn. "What a terrible way to spend your visit." She dropped her hands in her lap.

"It's okay," I said, sitting down next to her. "I like this kind of thing. I just decluttered my own place." It had been six months since Miranda moved out—a good time to cull my possessions. I had liked how it made me feel light and streamlined, like I was sharpening my life to a point.

"Oh, I hope you didn't throw out everything," she said, looking stricken. "I hope you kept your nice clothes. Your white blouses and things like that. The classics never go out of style."

"I didn't throw away any blouses," I said carefully.

That night, I carried my suitcase to my childhood bedroom. I checked my reflection in the mirror on the small vanity. Flannel shirt, no makeup, green hair with dark roots. I ran a finger across the vanity's surface. It was in pristine condition, even though Mom bought it when I turned twelve, but I'd barely used it and the paint was still pristine, eighteen years later.

I thought about texting Miranda. She was one of the few people who'd met my mother and would appreciate the comment about the blouses. I hadn't owned a blouse since the summer I'd worked as a caterer in college.

My mom never had a great grasp of who I was. Sometimes, when I was with her, I'd get the feeling that she wasn't seeing me, but someone else entirely.

I used to think there was something about me that brought it out in people. Miranda used to talk at me like I was a mirror, something to reflect her cleverness. I once had a boss who directed all her words six inches above my head. But my mom was the only person who added the coup de grace of invented details. Of seeing something that was vivid in her mind, and invisible to everyone else.

It used to really bother me. But I'd been thinking a lot since Miranda left. Mom was getting older. So was I, for that matter. I had one goal for this trip: to not fight with her. So I put my phone down and tried to let it go.

***

I woke up thinking about the woman I'd seen in the basement. After breakfast, I drove to the big-box hardware store and grabbed the first carbon monoxide detector I saw. I got labels and packing tape, too—proper tools for a proper declutter.

"The smoke is unbelievable," I said to the goth girl at the checkout counter. She was cute, with long, dark hair and arms covered in tattoos. "Guess you're all sold out of air purifiers and stuff?" She gave me a blank-eyed stare that said *Why are you talking to me,* but I didn't mind. No one hires a goth to be friendly.

Mom frowned when I pulled the carbon monoxide detector out of the bag. "Just to be on the safe side," I said. "CO_2 can build up when you're keeping all the windows closed. I saw it on the news." I didn't tell her about seeing the woman. I didn't want to worry her.

The display on the detector showed forty parts per million. Higher than usual, due to the smoke, but well under what you'd need to hallucinate.

I returned it and bought another. The goth girl rang it up without comment. There was something about her that made me want to hang around, but I didn't know what to say.

The new detector gave the same result. I kept seeing the woman in the basement. Every couple of hours, I'd enter a room and she'd exit, like figures on a cuckoo clock. I'd only catch a glimpse of her, but each time she looked the same. Dark hair, cut straight across the nape of her neck. A maroon skirt. And a crisp white blouse that glowed in the basement's dim light.

She moved silently. Of course she did, I told myself. She's not real. On the third day, I googled *can wildfire smoke make you hallucinate*

***

My mother wasn't aware of the woman, as far as I could tell. But sometimes, when we talked, her gaze would sharpen and drift to the side, like she was watching something. I'd glance over my shoulder and see a flash of white.

"What are you looking at? You keep spinning around."

"Nothing," I said. "I thought I saw a mouse."

That night, Mom started to look agitated, her eyes darting around the room as we watched TV. I wondered if I'd disturbed the woman. I wanted to text Miranda about it, but I didn't know what to write. I slumped lower on the couch and looked up signs and side-effects of mold.

***

On the fifth day, she left me a message. It was written in greasy pink cursive across the vanity mirror: LEAVE.

The woman had handwriting like a primary school teacher, clean and controlled. There was a lipstick tube on the vanity, cap on, blunted stick carefully swivelled back inside. I checked the colour. Cherries in the Snow.

I cleaned the glass with a tissue, wiping carefully so I wouldn't stain the white-painted frame. I could smell pancakes cooking downstairs.

I googled *how to get rid of a ghost* and read my phone while I ate.

We spent the day like we did all the others, sorting and piling and filling the car with donations for the thrift store.

"I can't believe you saved perfume," I said, pulling a squat, gold-topped bottle out of a box. "This has all got to go."

"Save that! I love White Shoulders!"

"It says White Linen."

"White Shoulders, White Linen, you know what I meant."

"But which one do you want to save?" I tried not to sound annoyed. She was doing that more now—saying one word when she meant another.

137

"All of it," she insisted. "No, the whole box."

"It's probably expired," I said sourly. I was quiet after that. I was thinking about what I'd read online, and putting together a plan.

That night, I waited until mom went to bed, and then I waited some more, watching TV with the volume turned down low. When I was sure she was sleeping soundly, I stood in front of the hall mirror—the biggest one in the house—and wrote HELLO on the glass with Cherries in the Snow.

I tried to write neatly, but my printing was an unsteady scrawl compared to hers. Underneath, I wrote LET'S TALK.

I stood there for ten minutes, watching the mirror. I didn't know how long to wait, or even what I was waiting for.

The house was so quiet I could hear mom's bed creak as she rolled over. Her room was just down the hall. I'd chosen this spot because I didn't want to invite the presence into my bedroom. But now I started to feel exposed. What would I do if mom woke up?

I gave up. I walked quietly into the kitchen and grabbed the Windex from under the sink. When I stood up, something moved in the window above the sink. I stopped. My mouth went dry and sticky as I stared at the fuzzy reflection of the kitchen behind me.

The woman sat at the kitchen table, her legs crossed at the ankles. I glanced behind me. Nothing.

I looked back at the window. Still there. It was the first time I'd seen her head-on. Her reflected face was blurry—blurrier than everything around her. She had a red smear for a mouth, and two dark holes where her eyes should be.

"Leave," she said, in a voice that sounded like a drawer shutting.

"I'm not going to leave," I said, swallowing a spike of anxiety. "But I think it's time for you to go." I tried to keep my tone level. My google search said it was important to be friendly, but firm. Like a good bartender cutting someone off. "This is my mother's house now, so whatever business you have here is done."

"This is my mother's house."

I frowned. "What do you mean?"

"She brought me into being like she brought you into being."

The figure stood and started pacing. I suddenly felt very aware of the space behind me.

"Do you know how frustrating it was to almost have her love?" she asked. "You were always in the way, with your big, lumpy body."

"Hey now," I said.

"She refuses to look at me, she's so stubbornly rational. And you insisted on being seen, with your stupid hair and your tattoos." She spun on her heel, vibrating with malice. "You think you're invisible, but you loom large in my world. You blot out everything."

"Fuck off," I said.

I'd been standing with my belly pressed against the kitchen sink, Windex and paper towel in one hand. I tightened my grip on the bottle and closed my eyes. Then I turned and walked out of the kitchen in one quick movement.

For a moment, the air was thick with the smell of wax, flowers, and damp basement. Then I was through it and into the hall. The tips of my fingers touched the cool glass of the hall mirror. I sprayed it with Windex and breathed the chemical deep into my lungs. I stared at the carpet while I wiped the lipstick off. I didn't look up to check how well I cleaned it.

***

I woke up with a start the next morning. I glanced at the vanity, but the mirror was empty. Thank God.

I lay in bed and thought about what the woman had said. "She brought me into being like she brought you into being." Could my mother have a child of her mind? Did that make the woman my sister, or was just a part of my mother projected into the world? Was there even a difference between those two things?

I grabbed my phone and typed Miranda a long email. Then I deleted it. Stupid. You can't message your ex about ghosts in your mother's basement.

But maybe it helped a little, because when I went to the return counter at the hardware store that afternoon, the words were right there.

"Again?" The goth girl nodded at the box in my hands. "Don't tell me that one didn't work either."

"I'm not sure," I said, putting the carbon monoxide detector on the counter. It was the third one I'd bought that week. I liked that she'd been keeping track. "It probably works fine. But not for what I'm dealing with."

She frowned.

"I think my mom's house might be haunted," I said. "Do you have anything for that?"

Her face froze.

"I'm not, uh, I'm not kidding," I said.

140

"Are you asking me because of the way I look?" She crossed her lovely tattooed arms.

"No," I said, weakly. She looked skeptical. I pointed at a big orange banner that hung behind the service counter. "I'm looking for Honest Help with all my Home Problems," I joked.

She sighed and started processing my return. She didn't look at me.

"Please," I said, leaning forward. "I'm sorry. I'm not teasing you. I'm asking because I don't live here and I don't know anyone and I don't have anyone else to ask."

She glanced up. "And for the record," I added, "I like how you look."

She considered me for a long moment. I didn't rush her.

"I might know someone," she said finally. "Give me your number."

***

The goth girl's name was Carolina. I texted her everything that had happened. She replied a few hours later with instructions from a friend. *I don't know much about this stuff but Dani thinks you have a brood parasite.*

??????

An entity that's attached itself to your family. Like a cuckoo. They lay their eggs in other bird's nests

I shivered.

Carolina's friend said to stick a candle to the bottom of a jar. I found a jar in the recycling and an old, pink-striped birthday candle in the back of the junk drawer. That night, I stayed up late again. I stood in the kitchen with my back to the sink, took a deep breath, and lit the candle.

I leaned against the sink and watched the shadows flicker across the cupboards.

I was supposed to wait until the candle was almost burned out. It didn't take long. When the candle was down to its last half-inch, I screwed the lid on tight. The presence would be attracted to the energy of the flame, Dani said. And once I put the lid on, it would be trapped.

The flame wavered as the oxygen ran out, then sputtered and died. I held the jar up to my face, looking for a sign.

The jar split with a loud crack. There was a whoosh of hot air, like I'd just opened an oven door. The smell of hot wax and flowers washed over me. I shrank against the heat and braced myself for whatever would come next.

But nothing happened. I opened my eyes and stood up slowly. The floral smell started to ebb. The jar was warm in my hands, held together only by the lid. I put it gently in the sink.

I heard a thump from somewhere else in the house, some place close.

"Oh fuck," I said softly. Now I'd really pissed her off.

I crept into the hall. I could hear shuffling sounds coming from my mom's room. I flicked on the hall light.

"Mom?" I whispered. "Is that you?"

Her bedroom door was ajar, the room beyond dark. I peeked inside. The bed was empty, but I could hear her moving around.

"Mom," I said again. "You okay?" I pushed the door open a little more.

I saw the flash of something pale—her hand, I think. And then she staggered into the patch of light thrown by the door. She was lurching, spinning, her arms stretched out.

I turned the bedroom light on. She didn't stop. Her eyes were wide open, staring at nothing.

I glanced at the window. In the reflection, I saw the woman. She was dancing face-to-face with my mother, holding her arms and whirling her around. Her skirt flared around them as they spun.

"Mom," I said urgently.

She turned her head, but looked right through me.

"Let's get into bed," I said softly. I approached her from the side and put my hand on her arm. I tried to ignore whatever the woman was doing around me. I could smell wax and flowers—lipstick, I thought.

I pulled my mom onto the bed. She felt so soft and boney under my hands. Light as a child. I pulled the covers up to her chin. Suddenly, she flailed, knocking the blankets away. Her bony knuckles caught me right under the eye. I jerked back. She punched and scratched at the air. I couldn't tell who she was aiming at.

"Shhhhhhh," I said. "Ignore her." I leaned out of striking range and stroked her hair. I did that until her hands stilled and her eyes closed.

I slid my phone out of my pocket. *didn't work* I texted. *cuckoo is still in the nest.* I looked at my mom. Her face looked peaceful. *sorry for texting late* I added.

***

143

I woke up with my face pressed against my mom's blanket. I rolled over. She was sitting up in bed, frowning at me.

"Did you sleep here?" my mom asked.

I sat up. "I didn't mean to. You were sleepwalking. Do you remember?"

"I was not," she said indignantly. "I've never sleepwalked a day in my life. What did you do to your face?"

I touched my cheek and winced. "You were sleep-fighting, too."

"I was not." She looked affronted.

"Okay," I said. I was too tired to argue. I pulled my phone out of my pocket. There were seven messages from Carolina. Despite myself, I smiled.

Dani says you need to use a stronger trap. Do you live near running water?

That evening, I walked down to the creek. The air was hazy with smoke. The sun hadn't set, but the light was dim. I made my way down to the edge of the water and pulled a perfume bottle out of my backpack. I pried the sprayer off and dumped the contents on the gritty edge of the creek, gagging at the smell and apologizing to anything living downstream. I rinsed the bottle carefully in running water and sprinkled it with salt like Carolina had said. Earlier that day, I'd driven back to the hardware store, where Carolina had handed me a small cork.

"Dani made this for you," she said, pressing it into my hand. She gave me a searching look, like she was still trying to decide if I was delusional, or just unlucky. I didn't mind. I just wanted it to work.

144

I would follow Dani's directions again. It's not like I had a lot of options. But I'd started to think that Dani was wrong about one thing. The woman wasn't a parasite. She wasn't an outsider. I didn't know what she was, but I couldn't ignore how familiar she felt. Something about her tugged at me, and made me think of flipping through magazines when I was a child, the full-page perfume ads, all elegance and glamour. She didn't remind me of my mother, but of the kind of woman my mother admired. Wanted to be. Wanted me to be.

That night, I faced the hall mirror once again. I put the box of old perfume bottles at my feet and wrote on the glass.

LET'S MAKE A DEAL

She was there before I could put the cap on the lipstick, standing just behind my left shoulder. Her features weren't just blurred, but swirling. I caught the scent of crayons, dust, and rancid oil.

"You want me to leave," I said quickly, trying to look at any part of the mirror that wasn't her swirling reflection. "How about this—if you can pass my test, I will leave the house."

"Leave forever?"

"Yep."

"You want to trap me. You tried already." The murk of her eyes spilled across her face.

I crouched and pulled a bottle out of the box. I set it on the floor and stood up.

The red smear of her mouth slid towards my ear. "Do you want to see what I see when I look at you?" she whispered in a voice like clinking silverware.

145

I was standing right in front of the mirror. I couldn't stop myself—I looked at my reflection. But I wasn't there. I'd been replaced by a lump, purplish and wrinkled, studded in eyes. No mouth, no limbs, and eyes all over, shiny and dark like dogs' eyes. The lump twitched like a giant tongue and all the eyes widened in alarm.

"Don't be scared," she said. "That's you. The real you."

Something moved in the mirror behind us. It was my mom, shuffling towards the bathroom in her yellow pajamas.

"You are all eyes and she has none," the woman whispered. "I know her so well." Her breath was hot on my neck.

"If you can fit in the White Shoulders bottle, I'll leave," I said, low and urgent.

"Promise?" she said, in a voice like creaking floorboards. "What did you do to it?"

"Nothing," I hissed. "Promise." She seemed to stare at me for a moment. Her features streaked. Then her body slid sideways, warping, looping in on itself until she was a narrow ribbon of colour. She slithered into the bottle like an eel. As the last inch of her disappeared, I dropped to my knees and jammed the cork in the bottle's narrow mouth, pushing hard to make sure it stayed.

"What on earth are you doing?" said my mother, flipping on the light.

"Nothing!" I said, too loudly. I spun and faced her, clutching the bottle close to my chest. I was afraid it was going to explode or burst into flames or something, but I was more afraid that my mom would let the presence out. I could feel my pulse pounding in my fingers.

My mother squinted at me, her face puffy and pillow-creased. "Why are you playing with the White Shoulders in the middle of the night?" She sniffed. "It smells funny in here."

"It's White Linen," I said. "You always forget." I inhaled, but the scent was already fading.

"Stop spraying that stuff and go to bed," she said, shuffling towards the kitchen.

I went upstairs and texted Carolina. *Some wild things happened but I think it worked. I think it's trapped*

omg!!!!

I sent her a photo of the bottle, even though it didn't look very impressive.

Dani says bury it in the yard.

I'll do it in the morning. Need to make sure it doesn't come back.

Bury it and then come tell us how it went. Dani wants to meet you.

I smiled. Then I glanced at the mirror on my childhood vanity. The purplish lump looked back at me, its hundred eyes shining with excitement.

***

I didn't think I'd ever fall asleep. But I must have because I woke the next morning to a clear summer sky.

"I'm so sad the smoke didn't clear 'til the end of your trip," sighed my mom as she buttered her toast. "But you'll get to see the sun for a day, at least. Maybe we should go into town."

"I was thinking of staying for an extra day or two," I said. "Maybe do some yard work. How would you like a flowering shrub outside the kitchen window? I've been talking to Carolina at the hardware store about it."

"Is that what you've been doing at the store?" My mom asked in a knowing voice. "You've been there every other day since you got here."

I felt a blush creep up the back of my neck. I didn't think she'd noticed.

"Just make sure you brush your hair before you go. Your bedhead is out of control."

I patted my hair. I'd tried to wet it and push it into shape, but I'd been going by feel. I didn't know if my normal reflection was ever going to come back. Good thing I'd never really gotten into makeup in the first place.

I looked at my mom. She wasn't wearing makeup, but she'd managed to put curlers in her hair, so her reflection must have been working fine. She seemed calmer that morning. Less distracted.

"Maybe I'll come with you," she mused. "See this friend from afar." She looked at me suddenly, staring intently at my face.

"What?" I said, fear tingling up my spine. I glanced at the kitchen window.

"I'm just thankful you came home," she said. "You've been really helpful."

"You're welcome." A new feeling stole over me. I didn't quite know what to do with it.

My phone buzzed. I grabbed it. It was Carolina: *Any more paranormal activity?*

Nothing I replied.

"Is that your new friend?" my mom asked. "You smile when you text her."

"Mom, stop," I laughed, covering my face with my hands. But I didn't stop smiling.

Stains
Nicoletta Giuseffi

Louise had come to dread that dreams she could not recall were the source of her anxieties.

Since she moved, her mornings were neither clouded nor shaded by phantasmic waking imagery, which lurked in all minds but rarely breached the skin between the subconscious and waking thoughts. The sun always came. Now that the soft-eyed thirty-something occupied another new apartment two thousand miles from her former life, where heavy snows replaced the rains she knew, she blamed the dreams she didn't remember instead of the distance, the stress, and the pain of leaving Carla. She couldn't bear to think it was a tangible circumstance which caused her migraines, her nausea, and her distraction. Already, the yolk of her thoughts had begun spreading in all directions from a cracked egg; she always failed to focus on anything.

She decided she had enough intrusive, nonconsensual reflection in the moments before she cast off the bed sheets. She carried herself from bed to the cramped, yellowing bathroom—a grad-student's only respite.

Louise still didn't know what transpired between her ears on any night since she arrived. This comfort, doled out by elements in her brain over which she had no control, did little to keep her hands from shaking when she looked into the mirror.

The glass betrayed thin yellow hair, eyes with luggage, and fluorescent skin like the buzzing halo of light overhead. She blindly fondled the items on the counter near the bathtub, grabbed something long and thin, and put her pink-tax razor in her mouth. Suddenly, she could imagine nothing save an inadvertent lurch slicing off her tongue. Racing thoughts had no qualms and no problems conjuring horrific images; they did her no favors. She could not help but imagine the hyperreal strawberry of her tongue falling out into the sink. Perhaps she spat it out herself to keep from choking on all the blood. It would wilt to grey as it emptied itself.

Louise slowly replaced the razor with her toothbrush, as it ought to be.

After she spat—white, she checked—she sat on her bed by the phone, picked up the receiver, and dialed Carla.

"Hello, this is Carla Zamora. I'm unable to come to the phone right now, so please leave a message."

Carla's voice, bright as the snow-occluded sun. The phone had cut off her smoky lower formants and she sounded even happier than before Louise left, but that couldn't be—the message was old—it was always that way.

Louise parted her lips as the phone issued a tone indicating recording.

"Hi Carlita, I miss you. I can't handle my advisor; she's cutting out all the parts of my thesis that really work. She doesn't think there's any reason to debrief the subjects, but I—sorry, that's—I should be talking about something else. I love you. You know, that dream I was having, I haven't had it again, but I'm worried that just means…"

A pause. Did she pick up? Louise fantasized contact and waited.

"Hello?"

Nothing.

"Sorry, I thought you picked up. Alright, remember before I left, I was having that dream about the stains? I haven't had it again since I got here. Let me back up. This is the dream where I wake up in my childhood room, when we both still lived in San Diego, remember? I find a stain on the floor, red jelly or something, wipe it up, get back in my bed, and go back to sleep. I don't know if I'm me, really me, in the dream."

She didn't know if she was her present self or her past self—the girl who sacrificed the prospect of ever having friends in school because she liked kissing girls more than anything. Even the smallest displays of love—a kiss next to the lockers, a held hand, a note in class—were hammered down because they weren't straight.

Twenty years hadn't changed that as much as she hoped. Carla still couldn't be her wife, and not for lack of trying.

"I kept having that dream," Louise continued, her tone level and hushed, like she didn't want someone to hear. "I woke up, saw the first stain, and wiped it up. The next night, I noticed there was another further away. I followed it. I left my room by the third night. The fourth, I found a stain on the stairs down from the landing. By the end of the first week of this, I was outside the house and turning left on Washington street where we used to climb that oak tree. I'm exhausted in the morning when I wake up from these dreams, and the nights I don't have them, I really worry. I worry I'm still having them and I can't remember. I'm finding more stains and I worry I won't have time to wipe them all up."

Louise stopped, and lowered the phone from her ear.

"Sorry, love you. I'll call later."

The thread of their connection severed, Louise lay on the bed and felt her senseless guilt straddling her throat. She couldn't tell Carla the rest—that there had been someone else in the dream. She couldn't see them, couldn't hear them, but the ancillary details had been filled in by her subconscious as though they were in the program they had given her in the lobby of the theater of the mind.

The feeling fouled the skin on her arm even sitting there on the bed. In the dream, she was wiping up the stains while someone observed her. The trail of gelatinous red smears were breadcrumbs leading her somewhere significant. She was hopelessly lost in an enervating ritual as she crouched, bent her back, and used a rag to ceaselessly wipe until the rag was saturated. It dripped with viscous red and oozed when she squeezed it—until she awoke and her arms were sore.

Louise couldn't bear the bed any longer. As she recalled the details of the dream, its dread poisoned the sheets and the pillows were capable only of asphyxiation. She drew herself up again and considered locking the bedroom door and sleeping on the couch, but that was where she had made her office, where she kept her notes, and where she had hooked a Gateway computer into the wall and set it on the flimsy coffee table.

The manila box was still humming. The monitor flashed images of red lips—her screensaver. She regretted it instantly.

Perhaps, she hoped in vain, attending to her e-mail first thing, instead of whiling away three hours doing things she pretended were more important, would help her shake the yoke of the yolk her anxious thoughts had become when her egg had cracked.

Click. Double-click.

There, waiting in her inbox, was a correspondence from her hovering spectral advisor, flagged *important* with a red exclamation point.

The living room, bathed in grey outside light, wilted beneath imagined heat. Louise mused over hypothermia, reminding herself of the snows outside, and how its onset imposed profuse sweating. When she downloaded and reopened the newly revised version of her thesis, only three days of an execution stay wherein the reply could have been affirmative, she followed a trail of red stains in highlighted text down, down, pages down, cut this, move this, change this, what is this, laughable, no time, revise, revise.

Louise began typing. A plate of the student dinner from last night—scraps of toast and a jar of preserves—waited invisibly behind her in the kitchen.

Re:re:re:re:re:re: Louise Wells – Thesis Draft Revision Final

Hello Margot,

Thank you for the prompt reply. I am reviewing your helpful suggestions. I still feel strongly that subjects will require a post interview wherein I debrief them on the goals of the study and the methods taken to ensure anonymity. We are asking a great deal of, may I note, students who are not being paid for their time. While the survey is helpful, I believe results cannot be useful without an additional qualitative element. Please let me know what you think.

Respectfully,

Louise Wells

Disengagement was the specialty of the grad student who survived to wear the regalia. She closed the navigator and turned to the stack of dog-eared papers from the control group wherein their dry, meandering reports on their dreams rarely raised her eyebrows. Half the subjects flew, one third of them met celebrities, and a vanishingly small amount produced any element of the remarkable or the unpleasant, beyond naked speeches. Still, she was too aware of the inequity at work. Funding was life and it was death. It had already killed her principles, but she would not let it kill her research.

The stack of papers could wait. The kitchen beckoned; her stomach, twisted in the knots of nausea she always seemed to suffer in the morning, split itself in half begging to be fed and pleading to be left well alone. Her hand drifted over the black-grout counter and brushed the plate of scraps against the open jar of raspberry preserves with seeds resembling insects suspended in the semisolid medium. The jar's harsh glass shattered at her feet. She looked down and felt the cool red jelly against her foot—seconds later, a shock of pain rode up her leg.

Feet planted, Louise crouched, bent her back, and dragged a rag from the oven handle. She squinted and made out the sparkling islands of glass in the sludge of red. A gaping cut ran down her ankle and fed into the pile of preserves—red on red—one bright and real, and one artificial food dye no. 40. Citric acid sizzled the cut, but she fixated instead on the stain, on the color—on how much it looked like what she had been wiping up in her dreams for the last few weeks before she moved to complete her final semester.

"Hello," she whispered. She felt compelled to say it. Words were awkward. In dreams, speaking was unnecessary.

The shards of glass were tooth-like, canine ridged. They formed into a mouth the longer she looked at them. She sopped up the mess with the rag, gathered up the glass where she could, and tiptoed to the sink to avoid splinters. She washed her hands and saw in the corner of her eye a smear of blood she had brought with her. The smear followed her back to the carpet and melted into the abrasive brown fibers all the way back to the bathroom, where she smothered its source in ointment and cursed as colorfully as her new wound bled.

The phone in the bedroom called out. Louise ambled over and collapsed on the floor next to the bed, afraid of the world suggested in the furrows of the pillows.

"Hello, Louise Wells speaki—"

"Hi darling," a grin answered her. Carla could be felt even over all that distance. "I listened to your message. Sorry about your dream. I had one about this big tree falling on me one time. You know you're going to finish and come back soon, yeah?"

"Hi, yeah, I know."

"But it's too easy to worry when you're alone."

"It is."

The conversation paused as they listened to each other's breath. It was subtle, barely audible, but it was something they did whenever they were so far away that the phone became the closest thing they had to being in the same room.

"How is the study going? Get any good ones?" Impish tones had wriggled into Carla's voice.

"One of the respondents has been dreaming about getting her period. She's pregnant, says she worries in the dream that it's not her period, but a stillbirth."

Carla's whistle carried through the phone and crackled.

"That's intense. I really feel for her. I wish counseling wasn't so stigmatized. Girl needs somebody to talk to."

"I cut myself open a minute ago."

"What?"

"Oh—just an accident in the kitchen. But I knocked over a jar of jam and saw my stains again. The glass was sitting in it and sticking up like teeth. I never noticed that before."

"Before what?"

"That's how it looks when I'm dreaming. I remember now."

"Poor thing. Write it down or something, yeah? Listen, I have to go to the clinic, early shift. You be good, okay?"

They exchanged love-yous and cooed and fawned for a moment longer, then the connection again was severed. The silence crashed in waves against the walls; it bled through the bandage on Louise's ankle, and jailed her in a bleak cell of months alone she had to believe would end.

After a few hours re-reading respondents' papers with the pervading buzz of the computer for company, Louise fell asleep nestled in the grey corduroy sectional. She dreamed again. An instant ninety minutes of black collapsed into the vivid white of the alley outside and the park beyond, inundated with falling snow. The grey corners of buildings cut straight lines into the strange curves of piled snow. Louise shuffled toward an empty bus following a trail of red stains—splatters in the snow, fresh and steaming.

As she approached the bus, her eyes followed the stains which sat atop the snow as light as air while her boots sank up to the knee. She passed one circular smear of red, still warm, with the cut blossom of the end of a tongue sitting in the middle.

The doors of the bus were a fan folded closed to open the way forward. The windows each were open shapes of broken glass and snow piled on the seats in heaping forms like riders, although all of them were no one. There was a red stain on every step, sparkling with glass shards. Louise had no rag, so she removed her cotton parka. She was immune to the cold; she did not feel it in the dream, and so she wiped and wiped at the stains until the parka's tan color had given way to red and crunched with accumulated shards of the invisible visible. The glass cut her hands, but she bent her back and worked as quickly as she was able.

The someone in her dream had always been chasing her. She had spared Carla that detail. She dared not turn her back because she felt them, or it, floating above her shoulders waiting for her to take notice. Each time she worked until the last stain was sopped up, and then she awoke. Yet, in the last dream before she left Carla again, she had felt a pair of hands and an open mouth behind her although she did not turn. Through the logic of dreams, she knew this implicitly, and she feared it. She only barely wiped up the last stain she could find while it reached for her.

Now there was no waking state to save Louise. The dream was everything when she was in it, and outside its endless confines, there existed nothing. Inside, every moment and every quaking anticipatory firing of neurons sent fear down dendrites and further until it spilled out of her hands and froze her mouth. Anxiety pulsed in waves from the stain she hadn't managed to clean off the floor of the bus. It stared up at her between her knees, glass teeth on teeth in layers rising up and many-fingered hands revealing themselves in the jellied tributaries of the red splatter.

The weeks had not been kind to the dream's landscape. She had moved and it had followed her in secret, occurring each night in her new apartment but disappearing before she awoke. It misled her across the country and now the trail grew longer than she could manage. There was no hope of earning one more day before the chasing, angry, unimaginable pursuer caught up to her. It was there now with her.

The stains were given form in it. It was every mouth; it was every open face of carved off limbs. Its whole was red jelly—blood jelly—embedded by a hundred angles of glass and speckled through with dots of dead vermin. The whole of the exit bowed out to accept its advance.

It reached for her.

The sounds in dreams were not sounds. There was no music, there was no speech, there were no vibrations. Instead of waves against ear drums, these were sparkling confections of the mind. They wove their way in and out of the brain's language centers, plumbed Broca's area and sang in a thousand tones out of time which were at once anticipated and known and recalled.

"Hello."

There were unsettling facts which she knew in the dream would happen to her, and are happening, and did happen.

Dinner Date
Anastasia Dziekan

"So, your profile says that you're a dog person?"

It seemed funny at the time.

"Yes, it does. I suppose I am." I clarify, "I don't have any pets of my own. I've just always preferred them to cats."

It's true enough that I don't keep pets. I can't—or rather, won't. They're mainly concerned with being fed. So am I. It doesn't mesh well.

"Me too!" She says this like it's some kind of amazing revelation. "When I was a little girl, I always wanted a pet poodle."

Well. You didn't get a poodle, Sarah. I mean, if her name actually is Sarah. She looks like the pictures on her profile. Strawberry blonde with blue eyes and freckles. She dresses cutely in mainly light pink. She takes her coffee with so much milk and sugar that it's practically white. It was my idea to meet at the local coffee shop. It's in public. It's daylight. I speak the language; I play nervous. "You never really know who you're meeting when it's someone from an app," I text, and it puts me in the position of the one who's scared. It puts her on defense and makes her have to prove to *me* that she is safe. And she does a good job of it. She looks… cartoonishly innocent. Fairy tale girl wandering into the woods innocent. With pink lips and doe eyes. And a cute laugh that never gets louder than a giggle. It's nice—for now.

"I had fun today," she says, with a smile that crinkles her nose.

"So did I." And I'm not lying.

"So," she bites her lip. "Are we... maybe on for a second date?" She bounces on her heels when she talks.

"I think so, maybe, yeah." Practice suggests that just a little bit of playing hard-to-get yields good results in the long term. "I'll text you."

No more than a few days pass before plans are solidified and we meet again. I take her out somewhere a little fancier. It's a nice restaurant, but not so nice that they look at you weird if you ask to take a lot of your meal home in a doggy bag.

"I'm just not very hungry tonight, that's all. And I like saving leftovers."

Her eyebrows lower slightly. "I understand." She seems to feel the need to be more sympathetic because she almost stutters as she adds, "I mean, that was pretty filling stuff. And I, uh, I never really met a girl who liked steak that rare."

I laugh lightly. "I guess I'm not really like most girls."

She's still looking at me, and I can't quite read her expression.

"Oh no, did I freak you out? Your profile doesn't say you're a vegetarian, but if you are, I—"

"I'm not,' she cuts me off with a gentle hand on my arm, "I just think you're gonna lose a lot of that flavor and stuff when you heat it up in the microwave."

"Oh, right, yeah. I've done it before. I know the right way."

Raw.

Raw out of the fridge with my bare hands and teeth.

On desperate nights when I make promises to myself.

On desperate nights when I can hear the deer outside in the nearby woods and I want to curse them for being so damn fast and messy.

When I am willing to take anything that can fill my stomach so long as it keeps me sated for just long enough to send a breakup text and block a number.

That's the *right* way.

"It's about timing," I say.

She nods. I'm about to start saying goodbye when she says, "Hey, I should probably walk you home."

"I don't live far from here. I wouldn't want you to walk away from your car and have to circle back just to take me a block."

"I used a rideshare. I can call it from anywhere. And besides, on your profile you were all worried about meeting someone. Totally, *totally*, valid by the way! It doesn't seem right to let you go home in the dark alone. I mean that's, like, way scarier. At least to me. Who knows who could be wandering around at this time of night?"

I blink.

I squint at her.

I honestly think I may have tilted my head.

"Oh, sorry," she backtracks, hands moving almost panickedly, "I didn't mean to scare you. And here you were worried about freaking me out and then I go and talk about how there could be murderers in the dark! Like, I'm trying to comfort you and then I do that!" She stops waving her hands and instead grabs at her hair like she's frustrated at herself. I catch a quick glimpse of her actually biting her lip, and I presume it's to physically keep her from rambling. It's cute. It's *really cute*.

"Hey."

She looks over at me, all wide-eyed.

"You didn't scare me. It's sweet of you to offer. We can walk together if you want."

She smiles like she just unwrapped the doll she's been begging for on Christmas and links her arm with mine, and then we're off.

I do not think about how the stillness of the night air lets me hear her heartbeat.

I do not think about how if she had bit her lip just a little bit harder, she would have drawn blood.

She whispers, "I'll let you in on a secret—I wanted to walk with you to keep you safe, but mostly I just wanted to spend time with you."

She kisses me goodnight.

I think about how she tastes like vanilla.

The next morning, I am near manic, and I start to make deals with myself. I could survive, I rationalize, on leftover steak. And maybe on the deer that live in the woods near me, and yes, they are gross and no I won't be able to take much back with me, but deer die all the time. Get hit by cars and whatever and it's fine, no one questions it. People question missing girls—they do. And it's easy to blame it all on internet dates gone wrong. And who doesn't bring their phone to a date these days? And you can do a lot to remove evidence by running a factory reset. And it's easy, they make it so easy—*too* easy.

I am hungry.

Hunger is usually the first sign.

The calendar mocks me from its spot on the wall. I have about a week before there's nothing left to fight against. Just me and the moon. Me and my instincts. No way to blame it on some separate entity inside of me. Some urge, some demon I need to defeat. Just me—inhuman and feral—and whatever's in my way.

The day passes fitfully. I jump every time I hear my phone buzz. I send her enough texts to reassure her that I'm alright. I ask her about her day. I send her a picture of a poodle I saw a couple days back. When she sends back a row of heart emojis, I consider throwing my phone across the room just to see it explode into pieces against the wall.

I think about her.

She's soft and gentle—and *kind*. She's trusting in the way most girls aren't on the second date. It's like she's willing to project love into the world, even knowing the damage it could do to her.

I think about dirty deer.

I think about running through the forest, wild beyond the point of reason, not caring when I cut through brambles and thorns until I wake up the next morning covered in scratches and bruises and blood that is not mine. And it doesn't even taste good.

The solution, I know, is that if I really love her so much, I should break up with her. Cut myself from the temptation entirely.

I force myself not to indulge logic and will myself to sleep.

The next day, I plan.

I can't have her like that, and I won't go for dirty deer and raw steak, so it'll have to be someone else.

Someone... not as good.

I log back into the app, delete my old profile, and make a new one. Last time, I used the name Joanne and this time, I decide to be Kara. The name doesn't mean much, just as long as I don't use my real one. Makes it harder to track me.

Then I go through my photos, trying to choose the best set. There's an order I go by—a normal one first, where I just look pretty, and then the next one is a bikini picture—not too risqué, but the kind of thing I know works—and a photo that has at least one other person in it. It shows that I am normal and have friends (even if that's a lie), and then I add one more photo relating to one of the interests I'll end up listing—to show I'm not faking it.

I fill out the rest, answering the stupid little questions it asks me. I quickly become annoyed, frustrated that I have to go through this again. Especially when I've already done all this work and haven't enjoyed the benefits yet.

It's the anger that comes after the hunger.

There's only a few days left until things are beyond my control. The night will pass as it passes. There will be no time to be rational, to pause and think things through. I can plan as much as I want until *the* moment. But when the moment comes, it cannot be stopped.

My phone buzzes.

It's a text from Sarah:

Dinner Date

"Hey, did your profile disappear? I can't find it :("

Something in me churns bitterly. I think for a second that I am caught. I clench my jaw as I try to steel myself enough to reply: "I deleted it. Figured I didn't need it anymore since I have you"

"Aww! That is SO sweet of you!"

And then suddenly—irrationally—I am angry at her. For not being smart enough to realize something is up. For not getting away, for not saving herself. For not running. She's making it easy. Why does she have to make it easy? Why can't she be the hero, leave me alone, and take the choice out of my hands?

"BTW when can we go on a date again?"

I don't have a chance to calm down before I type, "Friday? My place?" and hit send.

"It's a date!"

I know what night that is. I know what I've set in motion.

Rage still storms in my stomach as I go to the kitchen to start preparations.

When she comes over, the table is already set. The tablecloth is red, and I chose it on purpose. I did cook, but I don't eat much of it. I gravitate toward the meat, of course, but still I barely pick at it despite how hungry I am.

"Are you alright?" She asks from the other end of the table. "You look kind of upset."

My stomach rumbles.

"I'm fine."

She hesitates. "I—*are* you? I mean, I didn't pressure you into this date or anything, did I?"

Still so insecure. Nervous. Anxious. Where's the confidence that let her walk me home down dark streets? She thought I couldn't fend for myself, and what—she'd fare better? I couldn't fend off an attacker but her—barely 5'2" in heels—could save my life? How weak does she think I am? How safe does she actually feel? She thinks nothing can go wrong for her.

"Jo?" I realize I've been staring off into space, lost in thought. "Should I not have come?"

The pity I feel for her twists in my gut. The words escape her like a whimper. She sounds so sad, so helpless, so *wounded*. And that's—well, those are the deer in the forest that the hunter goes for, y'know? Deep down, I don't think anyone wants to be the one to kill something innocent, but that doesn't ever cancel hunting season. I almost want to laugh at myself for getting attached. For playing with my food. I'm angry at her for making me doubt. Forever thinking I could throw it all away and starve for her.

A low growl rumbles in the back of my throat when I smile at her. "No, Sarah, you shouldn't have come."

And then it's paws on the table, leaping over it, full speed tackling.

It's shoved to the ground—the feeling of teeth biting down—body transforming with every movement, stretching and contorting into a beastly figure.

It's her screaming, plates shattering, and blood seeping into my dining room floor.

It's chaos and noise, and my vision fading into black and white like old grainy photographs.

And then I black out.

When I come to, I am me.

Dinner Date

I am lying on the floor, panting, still trying to catch my breath. The scene around me is pure destruction.

I force myself to look at what's left of Sarah.

I try to evaluate how much of her I can fit into the plastic take-home boxes from that restaurant.

The White Room

Annabeth Leong

All Angela Baker ever did was sit in a white room and talk.

According to the therapeutic methodology favored by the director of the Raymond Dunway Home, a social worker like Angela should be listening more than talking—but honestly, her patients frightened her, and so she barely let them get a word in edgewise. This prevented them from telling her the specifics of their nightmares, which had a tendency to then become her own.

She talked about all sorts of things related and unrelated to psychotherapy.

She explained various approaches to psychotherapy—the organic holism of Gestalt therapy, Albert Ellis and Rational Emotive Behavior Therapy, how Hyman Spotniz extended Freud's theory of psychoanalysis to enable the treatment of people with borderline conditions of psychosis—but did not attempt to use any of these techniques with her patients.

When she ran out of graduate school topics to regurgitate, Angela turned desperately to the news, describing everything from which celebrity had a bad case of acne to the latest refugee crisis, all under the pretext of 'keeping her patients informed about the outside world.'

She did not talk about herself, and certainly not her own nightmares. Despite her best efforts to drown out her patients' voices, Angela's dreams had become more frequent and more disturbing.

She rocked in her chair as she talked, plastic and metal squeaking beneath her. The chairs at the Home were like the ones she'd used in elementary school—primary colors, sticky with the ghosts of unknown fluids. Sitting in them made her feel younger, unqualified, and vulnerable. She laced her fingers together in her lap to keep from worrying at her nails or sliding her fingertips over the chair's plastic seams, which were sharp enough to cut when touched at the right angle. The chairs had been made cheaply in a mold and no one had ever sanded them down.

When a patient did manage to verbally corner her into listening to something horrible, Angela usually could not maintain her preferred posture. Her hands escaped her control, and she ran her fingertips over the plastic seams under her chair until she bled, the distraction of the stinging pain enough to ward off a few more unwanted sentences.

She tried not to look at her patients or notice any of their identifying features. They were a parade of names with a single diagnosis, and she intentionally blurred them into one amorphous shape, one mouth speaking words that Angela did not want to hear—one body that she had to sit with all day in a white room for fifty minutes at a time, with ten-minute breaks in between.

She tried never to look at, for example, Gloria Jackson's face, burned on the left side to the point that the flesh looked like boiled plastic and one eye squinted out from within the melted horror of her brow. Angela tried not to remember what Gloria had said about how it had happened, the angel who had visited her in dreams night after night since she was small, always speaking to her from afar until the night Gloria's mother died, when the angel drew her into an embrace that would have been comforting except its feathers were tongues of fire—its robes rivers of lava—its words the crackling of an inferno.

Angela tried never to look at the strong jaw of Charles Myers or his sensual lips. When he came to see her, he sat politely in his chair, his voice reasonable, his face calm. He listened patiently as Angela stammered through story after story about the election, natural disasters, and portions of the Amazon rainforest that were dying off forever—but if she paused even for a breath, he would speak to her about the Endless Man, the one who had kindly persuaded him to give up his soul.

"It's better without one," Charles Myers had said once when Angela couldn't think of anything else to say. At that, she'd made the mistake of looking him in the eye— ordinary brown, but meeting his gaze had felt like motion sickness, like nausea gathering below her belly button and moving upward toward her esophagus. It made her throat tighten, trying to hold back what her body wanted to vomit out.

Since then, she'd been careful to look at the walls instead of at the patients' faces. The walls were white, it was true—but staring at them for eight, ten, or twelve hours a day—Angela realized there was more to white than it seemed. There were shades of white. These walls weren't the rich, carefree white of a summer cloud nor the inviting, pristine white of a freshly cleaned sink at a luxury hotel. The walls of her office were the hard white of bone, glistening in some spots and yellowed in others.

It was like being inside a ribcage. She could feel the room and the Home expanding and contracting around her while she, the room's pounding, anxious heart, supplied whatever she could to make this all go on.

And then there were the cracks, the inevitable signs that everything comes apart eventually. She knew them all like friends, and traced them with her eyes day after day. Sometimes, the cracks threatened to form images, but Angela always pushed that away. *This is just a white room,* she told herself. *All I do in here is talk. There's nothing interesting to look at on the wall, nothing anyone says that I need to hear.*

But someone was talking to her—had been talking for a while. Instinctually, Angela drew in a breath, and ransacked her mind for a fresh topic to discuss. Fingers snapped in front of her face—elegant, manicured fingers. Not the hand of a patient.

Angela blinked and allowed the other person in the room to come into focus.

"Angela, what are you doing?" Iris Lawrence asked.

She was the daytime receptionist for the Home. She wore a slim winter coat over her A-line work dress and tennis shoes for the walk to the subway. A fashionable yellow purse was slung across her body.

She'd refreshed her makeup and redone her blonde hair, and the golden glow on her cheeks made her prettier than anyone at the Home had any right to be. She looked like someone who could leave this place behind her when she walked out the door.

"Aren't you going home?" Iris was saying. "I know I wouldn't sit in this room any longer than I had to."

"I was just leaving," Angela said, standing, and collecting her own coat off the back of the chair. Her knees felt stiff. As her center of gravity shifted, she realized she needed to pee. Her heart sank. She had no idea how long it had been since her last patient had left.

176

The White Room

Iris put her hands on her hips and twirled slowly, skirt flaring, as she examined the featureless room. It contained nothing other than the two chairs. Angela's notebook and laptop case leaned against the metal legs of one of them. A tiny row of windows at the top of the wall across from the door grudgingly let a little outside light break through their layers of mold and grime. A fruity, floral perfume emanated from Iris as she moved, making her presence in that place seem even more surreal.

"You don't have to leave it like this, you know," Iris said. "You're in here every day. You're allowed to decorate. Don't social workers put up posters? Like the one of the cat that says, 'Hang in there?'"

Angela rubbed the back of her hand across her face, still trying to pull herself out of whatever state she'd been in. She felt ugly and drab, lost and incompetent. When did people grow up and become put together like Iris? "I don't really know what I'd do to make it better," she said finally, in response to an expectant head tilt from the other woman.

Iris wrinkled her nose. "Anything would help this place. Pick up grocery store flowers on your way into work tomorrow."

"There's nowhere to put them," Angela said.

"It wouldn't hurt to get a table, too. But even if you leaned a bouquet against the wall, it would be an improvement." She lowered her voice to a stage whisper. "Everyone's afraid of you. You should do something to set them at ease."

"They're afraid of me?"

Before she could control it, Angela's mind flashed to the bite scars on Cora Parker's arms. It wasn't a dog that did it, she insisted whenever she had the chance. It was a creature she called the Myrna. Angela had never allowed Cora to describe it, though she had tried.

Angela would have thought that the patients would stay focused on the fears they already had.

Iris picked up Angela's notebook and laptop case, pressed them into her hands and took her by the elbow. "Here, come with me. It's 8 o'clock already."

Angela blinked. Her last appointment had been scheduled to end at 5:30. She'd arrived at work at 7 a.m. She didn't think she'd eaten lunch, but despite the time, she didn't feel hungry for dinner. She allowed Iris to pull her out of the room and into the Home's featureless white hallway.

"What are you still doing here?" Angela asked.

Iris smiled brightly. "I'm having an affair with one of the doctors. We just stay late and go into one of the examining rooms."

Angela's insides squirmed at the thought of being naked anywhere inside the Home, of being touched by any of its thin-lipped doctors.

Her feelings must have shown on her face because Iris sighed. "I know it's pathetic, but it's so much easier than dating."

"Sounds like it." Angela couldn't remember the last time she'd even tried to date. She spent most evenings after work trying to relax enough to go to bed—meditation, tea, breathing exercises, boring books, trashy shows—and eventually going into her bedroom and lying there, too afraid to close her eyes.

Some nights she stayed awake until her alarm went off. Other nights, exhaustion overtook her and sucked her into the world of her nightmares. Both kinds of nights were terrible in their own way.

Iris shifted her grip on Angela, propelling her past the darkened, silent reception desk with its mess of family photos and trinkets from island beaches.

There was a night receptionist, but she rarely used the desk and only barely answered the phone. She spent most of her time in the kitchen microwaving various permutations of noodles and cheese. Angela had run into her but never spoken to her. She thought she liked her, though she wasn't sure of her name.

Iris unlocked the main entrance. The door was old and so heavy that she had to let go of Angela and lean both hands against it to get it open.

The resulting blast of chill outside air tightened Angela's muscles and reminded her that she needed to pee. She hesitated, feeling socially awkward and also reluctant to go through the ordeal of the bathroom. But it had been hours—she didn't really have a choice. "I'll be right back," she said, breaking free of Iris. "Hang on."

Iris rolled her eyes but didn't leave.

Angela made her way back down the hallway to the staff bathroom. She passed the kitchen, where the night receptionist was streaming an episode of some reality show on her cell phone. Angela forced herself to press on past her.

She had to avoid thinking about the nightmares, or she'd never be able to walk through the bathroom door, lower her pants and pee. Obviously, that was doomed. Knowing she couldn't think about her nightmares only made them stronger.

The friendly sounds of the familiar show began to fade behind her. Angela continued down the dimly lit hall.

The Home's bathroom smelled institutional and not fully clean. She didn't want to give her nightmares reality—what she had listened to of the patients' stories told her more than enough about the dangers of reinforcing them. Still, she couldn't resist checking herself in the mirror.

She was still herself. Tired eyes, no lipstick, and a nondescript dress from Anne Klein. Not the other face she saw sometimes in a bathroom mirror in a dream. The face that wasn't Angela Baker at all.

Hands shaking, she went into a stall. She took down her pants. Everything was normal. Everything was fine.

Still, Angela didn't want to touch anything. She clenched her thighs to hover a few inches above the seat. She held her breath and counted off the seconds she had to be in the stall.

She knew the nightmares weren't real, but still she felt like it was a narrow and temporary escape that she wasn't transforming right now, the way she had seen herself change so many times.

Her skin wasn't sliding off her muscles and falling to the floor to let another body climb out of her body. She didn't have to look at the mess of it lying on the bathroom floor, blood blackening the tiles around it—more fragile than she liked to think about but also disturbingly coherent.

And she was thinking about it now and she couldn't stop herself. She was remembering the dreams, the sense of freedom and exultation in her heart as she toyed with the bladed, poisonous flesh that grew from her new limbs. That part of the dream felt sensual in the moment, the way she imagined a model would feel rising from a swimming pool, knowing how good she looked in a bikini. But even in the midst of the nightmare's spell, in the back of Angela's mind, her dreaming self recoiled, knowing what sorts of horrors that body was built for, and knowing how hotly she anticipated them.

The terror of Angela's nightmares didn't come from being burnt, from trading away her soul to the devil, or from being bitten by the Myrna. The terror came from *becoming* the devil. For some reason, it always happened in the bathroom. She couldn't go into one anymore without a thousand memories of dark becoming, nor without wondering what sort of person she really was inside.

She had taken much more toilet paper than she needed. She discarded the extra and fixed her clothes. She washed her hands in the sink and uselessly checked her hair—flyaways everywhere.

On the way out of the bathroom came the last horror—the tiny flicker of disappointment that the transformation was still only a dream.

"Did you fall in?" Iris asked when Angela returned. She was standing just outside the door, staring vacantly in the direction of the methadone clinic across from the Home. It was closed now, but the parking lot was littered with discarded plastic cups.

She had her phone in her hand, but she wasn't looking at the screen.

Angela shook her head. "You really walk from here to the subway every evening? In this neighborhood?"

Iris snorted. "If anyone did something to me, they'd be doing me a favor," she said. Something dark crossed over her eyes.

Angela wanted to interrogate her, but instead she said, "Let me give you a ride tonight at least."

Iris shrugged. "Thanks."

They walked in silence to the gravel parking lot. Angela was still trying to shake the echoes of the nightmares. Now that she'd left work, her focus had shifted from blocking out her patients' voices to blocking out her own. It never worked. None of it did. Despite her white, undecorated room and her resolute attempts to talk about anything and everything else, pieces of their stories seeped through.

The patients frightened her because she could feel whatever that other body was, moving within her as they talked. She could feel her urge to prey on them. She sometimes wondered if what they were seeing in these nightmares—these dreams so real that they resulted in debilitating physical and emotional waking effects—was her. She sometimes hoped it was.

Angela's car was the last one in the lot. Someone, probably from the methadone clinic, had keyed it during the day. Angela ran her finger over the marred paint. It reminded her of the chair's plastic seams.

"That sucks," Iris said, coming closer. She smelled so good.

Angela realized now that Iris was only put together on the outside. She was lonely and impossibly sad behind the makeup, the dress, and the perfume. Angela's training, though intended for social work, had also given her all the tools she could possibly need to manipulate Iris all the way into another dimension if she wanted to. The thought made her smile. She kept her head down to avoid revealing the inappropriate reaction.

"It's fine," Angela told her. "It's an old car."

She went around to the passenger seat and opened it for Iris. Their arms brushed as Iris got in and arranged her A-line skirt. The skin of her hands was slightly darker than her legs. Her legs were perfectly smooth—shaved that morning for the doctor, perhaps.

Angela thought again about her dreams of looking down on a dripping pile of discarded skin, how it looked stretchy and fatty and strange when separated from a body.

Angela got into the driver's seat. "Where do you live?" she asked.

"It's kind of a long drive," Iris said. "You can just drop me at the subway if it's easier."

"I don't mind. Tell me your address."

Iris did, and Angela's nightmares were so close to the surface now that the thrill of knowing it was unmistakable. Angela pushed down the fantasies of what she could do with the information. She entered Iris's address into her phone's maps app, started the car and began following the instructions.

It was harder and harder to hide from herself, no matter how long she spent each evening staring at her white walls. No matter how many achievements she earned in her meditation app.

"Do you ever think about working somewhere else?" Iris asked.

"I should quit," Angela said immediately. "It would be good for me."

"Why don't you?"

If she was honest with herself, Angela could answer that question. But she tried not to be honest with herself, tried not to let herself know about the part of her that fed on the pain, the part of her that exulted in the concept of nightmares as real as the ones her patients suffered.

"Why don't *you*?" Angela asked instead of being honest.

Iris glanced at her, the darkness in her eyes again. "I don't exactly make choices that are good for me."

"The Home is a terrible place."

Iris shrugged again. "I understand it. That's worth something to me."

Iris turned on the radio, but a commercial was on and Angela turned it off. She was enjoying the awkward silence, the way it felt to not be talking. Driving into the night toward Iris's home, Angela found she wanted to listen to Iris. She wanted to hear about her nightmares.

The streets were relatively empty, and Angela found herself disappointed by the lack of traffic. She slowed as much as she dared, prolonging the trip.

Iris rolled her window down, then up again. She fiddled with knobs and the fastenings of her purse. Angela watched it all from the corner of her eye as she drove, noting the moment that Iris's hands took on a slight tremble.

"You're not going to pick up grocery store flowers, are you?" Iris asked.

"I don't think it would change anything."

"We'd still be afraid of you," Iris agreed.

The White Room

Angela noticed that she said *we*, not *they*, and it burst through her heart like the confirmation that a crush likes you back. She savored the word and Iris's unease for the remainder of the drive.

She pulled into the driveway for Iris's building far sooner than she would have liked. Iris lived in an old house that had been divided into many tiny and oddly shaped apartments, each with a separate entrance. A jumble of cars were scattered around it—no one had bothered to designate where residents should park. It looked like no one in particular was responsible for common areas. The porch was in the advanced stages of rotting, and the yard was covered with neglected masses of dirty snow and the half-decomposed remnants of fallen leaves from autumn.

It was a dark street and the walk to the apartment door was even darker. Angela was tempted to cut off the headlights and the engine. She was confident she could convince Iris to let her inside. She knew something would happen if she did.

In her nightmares, she often had a little foreknowledge. It sometimes increased the terror of a dream to know what was coming and yet experience walking into it anyway. On the nights Angela fell asleep and dreamed, the same sequences often repeated. She'd walk into a bathroom and discover her true self, then wake just as she was about to realize the full delight of her terrible new form. Then the process would begin again. She'd be innocent Angela again, wandering the hallway of a school or a doctor's office or the Home or the DMV, just looking for a bathroom—but in the back of her head, she'd already know what she was about to become, what she already was.

This felt the same.

But Angela kept her hands where they were. The lights stayed on and the engine continued running.

As Iris opened the door to get out of the car, she hesitated and turned toward Angela. It was all in her eyes now, the vulnerability and defiance and knowledge and fear. "I meant what I said earlier," Iris whispered. "If anyone did something to me, they'd be doing me a favor."

Angela's stomach lurched. She was still fighting the things she dreamed about. But she darted her head forward and took Iris's mouth with a sudden kiss. She savored Iris's startled surrender. She knew without being told that whatever transgressive thrill Iris had gotten from the thin-lipped doctor, it was weak compared to this moment.

Angela gripped the sides of Iris's face. Her fingers played over Iris's cheekbones and jaw, then lightly traced the sides of her throat, just enough to feel the flutter of the vein. Angela thought about the wonder and disgust of the human body and all its many, separate parts. Iris shivered under her touch.

Then the kiss ended, and Angela forced herself to let go. "Maybe someday," she promised.

Fathomless Things
Avra Margariti

I find Thomae burying herself in the forest.

"No!" The scream claws out of my throat as she sinks through the dirt's root-choked entrails.

Grasping her heaving ribcage, I pull her out of the dark-edged hole. My lover's body is a dead weight in my arms while I stick my fingers down her mouth to drag ribbons of velvety moss free from her esophagus. Her tongue is stained viridian as she coughs. Betrayal and resentment dance in her narrowed eyes, their whites gone to parchment-yellow, blinking away bugs and other decomposers. At least she's alive. She hasn't left me yet, now that I'm finally found.

"Let's get you home," I say. Thomae lets me guide her, the fight draining out of her form, naked but for the fungi clinging greedily to her pores.

"I needed to go back," she says, her voice as small as the snails that curl in her hair. "At least the forest *wants* me. I can hear its thrumming call. All you do is deny me, Maria."

Her accusation sets the guilt roiling within my dark-matter Void. We stand at the edge of the forest, the white-and-blue paint of our cottage peeking in the distance through the foliage. I know it's my fault she's like this, at least part of it. I thought I was doing the right thing, months ago, when I unhinged my mouth and swallowed her whole.

187

Helping her carry the burden of herself, diluting her sadness through the vastness of my being, hushing the world's psychic resonance that always rings through her ears.

I thought wrong.

But perhaps I can give her *something*. Even though it's wrong, too. Wrong again.

"You know I can't swallow you." Not after last time, when Thomae didn't come back the same. Mad-eyed and haunted by the age-old nightmares I had once shoved inside me, out of sight and mind. "I won't. But I can take the edge off. Just until I find another way to help you."

"Oh, please." She grips me with beseeching, bruising strength. Jagged nails bite into the skin of my neck. They leave behind dried mud and pinpricks of blood.

I brush my fingers against Thomae's cheek. Pluck a beetle from her raven-nest hair, and lick the filthy tears from her crow-footed eyes. Then I take her hand and kiss the back of it, oh-so-gently.

I swallow my own bilious guilt before opening my mouth just a crack. A spectral bellow escapes me. I rein it in before it reaches subsonic frequencies. Suitably human for now, I smile at Thomae before biting down on moss-flavored flesh.

***

We met at a dyke bar—*La Belle et la Bête*—as these things often go. But unlike most cautionary tales, it wasn't the monster who first approached the beauty.

Thomae slid onto the sticky stool beside me. I sat at the bar and stared at my beer in silence, sloshing the amber bottle but never taking a sip. She grabbed it from my hand,

and brought it to her lips, painted tar black and oil-slick shimmery.

"Not drinking?" she teased with a demilune smile. "Afraid some beer might upset that ancient ecosystem inside you?"

I snatched the bottle back in trembling fingers and willed my death grip to unclench. *La Belle*'s proprietress had a rule: broken glass and you're banned for good. I needed that space, where I could watch people from a distance while I pretended to drink. I craved this connection to the modern world, no matter how feeble. It was good here, where I vicariously fed my voracious hunger and no one asked any questions. Until now.

"What are you talking about?" I asked, injecting venom through my voice. A warning. I stared at the bar's stained wood grain, yet still felt her eyes on me. Crawling all across my being, then boring right *through*.

"I can tell there's more to you," she said. "I have the gift, you know. People tried to beat it out of me, had me committed one too many times." Her fingers drummed a furious staccato against the bar before stilling altogether. "But I can see you still. The outline of you is right, the human skin, but it's all a hoax. You are a writhing mass of dark matter stretching inward for as long as the eye can see."

She didn't sound disturbed, but exhilarated. I caught her scent when she shifted near me—stars on the edge of being born, empires on the brink of collapse. So much potential, so much need inside her, all directed toward me.

"*I see you*," she repeated, wrapping her fingers around mine. "I'm Thomae, and you?"

"Maria," I said, the first name that came to mind. It was the most common name for woman-shaped beings around these parts where I had wandered after my most recent hibernation.

If I were smart, I would have vanished right then. But it had been such a long time since I last talked to a human, or any entity at all. Longer still since anyone could tell there was something monstrous about me in a capacity beyond animal fear.

I see you, Thomae had said, and my grip slackened around the bottle. My fingers tangled with hers.

That night, Thomae took me home through deserted roads and unkempt forest paths. She drove her motorcycle as recklessly as if she were racing the stars above. I clutched her tight, feeling peals of laughter or perhaps sobs undulate through her body. And when she kissed me later, it was with her mouth open coffin-wide, her breath echoing down my larynx, into the cavernous, wet well of my stomach.

In the bed of her cottage by the forest, I let Thomae's hands map out my endless borders and forgot to worry about everything inside me—the monsters and shipwrecks and stars I had once swallowed—spilling out. Just before we fell asleep, the cosmic thrumming of my skin temporarily soothed, she looked at me with her face sliced in half by sharp moonlight.

"You're a doorway," she said, "and I've never found a lock I couldn't pick."

***

Thomae sleeps in our bed, restless and feverish. At least she's no longer sleepwalking to the forest, eager to

190

fall into the burrows of wild beasts, rock fissures, and graves dug by her own fractured fingernails.

I am the beast she invited to her home all those months ago—the monster that never left, craving to be seen. Then, once I became familiar with Thomae's wildly oscillating moods, I wanted to take care of her.

I made sure she slept, ate, and showered. Kept her away from sharp objects, open flames. Felt my nature sublimate into a milder version of the creature born before time itself. My skin hunger slowly easing, my curiosity about humans and their world ever-growing.

I thought I was helping, when I agreed to swallow her into my Void.

Now, I inspect the bandage wrapped around Thomae's non-dominant hand, and make sure the blood from the wound hasn't seeped through. I kiss her forehead, an action I learned through films, to check her temperature. Sniff the room for signs of prickly-sweet infection.

She's brought the forest back with her. The lingering scent of decay. I wonder if there is another magical consciousness out there—one that she could sense through her gift—or if it's all wishful thinking. When I first roamed into town, I thought I felt an older, occult lifeline thrumming underneath timber and mortar. It's been quiet since I settled here. A false alarm, or a being hiding itself from me?

Thomae groans, and I halt the meandering meridians of my thought.

"Maria," she whispers, stirring in her sleep.

She needs me now, more than ever. I take her injured hand to my mouth for the second time today, and I kiss the stump where her pinky finger had been. I only took the very tip, chomping down as she moaned and writhed. Tears streamed from her eyes yet her voice said *don't stop, I'll kill you if you stop. I will kill you.*

I open my mouth just a fraction and breathe against the ember-hot tip of her missing finger. She stills immediately, her lips curled in a somnolent smile. I roll away from Thomae, toward the cooler side of the sheets, but her fever—her want—seems to permeate our bed and the whole cottage.

I step outside, needing to breathe the fresh air of the countryside. But even on the porch, close to the forest's fir-clad fringe, the cloying heat remains. It smells like the burning center of the earth. Like fathomless, needful things.

A rumble from within bends me in half. My hands fly to my stomach. All those things inside me—the galaxies I gobbled down as a weeping infant abandoned in the half-made world—then later, all the wreckage I devoured, the lava-spitting volcanoes and volatile alchemical elements, the radiation and infernal war machines, the liminal undertows and Milky Ways of abominations—I never once felt the need to purge them. Yet when I swallowed Thomae, my body rejected her even as she clung inside me, tooth and nail, scratching bloody my mouth's pink human facade.

At least I can give her this comfort, even if it's only a compromise. The segment of pinky will help her feel connected to the space inside me, like a phantom limb or a placebo.

Except, as I trudge up the porch steps after one last glance at the unmoving mound of the forest, I feel another pang in my stomach, sharper than before. I fall to my hands and knees near the screen-door meant to keep out the forest and its creatures. I hack up through my throat's convulsive movements, the tip of Thomae's pinky. Give birth to her the way the universe once spat me out before humans had finished gestating inside its gut—a lonesome, furtive teratogenesis.

Quickly, I grab a bucket and mop, and soak up the evidence of my sickness. I hide away the pinky finger. Proof of how, once more, I have failed the one I was never supposed to love.

***

Thomae rode her motorcycle fast and wild, kissed strangers more monstrous than I could ever be, and got into fights and stuck sharp objects—old needles and broken beer bottles—through her thin skin. *La Belle et la Bête*'s proprietress had long since banned us both for life.

"It's so loud," Thomae would cry, coming home covered in bruises and other women's fluids. "The world, its thrumming echoes. Can't you hear them? People tried to beat the gift out of me but they only made it stronger. Impossible to switch off."

She clutched me closer and shoved me away in equal measure when I cleaned her body and dressed her wounds. She changed her tune when she took her psych-prescribed pills. Coiled around me tight in bed, buried her face in the crook of my neck. Closer, deeper.

Never, ever enough.

"Can't you feel it?" she would ask. "This energy between us? How I wish I could crawl inside you and never come out? How we would be one, and I'd be free?"

I imagined what she was asking for. Having Thomae inside me in the last remaining way she hadn't yet gotten under my skin. I could manifest teratoma eyes in the lining of my stomach and watch Thomae float through my darksome, soundproof sea, all of life's worries briefly forgotten. She was the one who taught me about human concepts such as subspace, meditation, and memory palaces. I wanted to give her this. The pills kept the world's psychic resonance at bay, but they also made her forlorn and lethargic. The rest of her escape routes—the running away from her ghosts only to circle back into their arms—far too reckless.

So I kissed Thomae and said, "Yes. I can feel you. I can take the pain away."

I pulled away from her clinging embrace only to open my mouth as wide as it would go. The human facade I had learned to weave out of the ether fell away, the skin around my mouth stretching like the special effects wax in Thomae's monster films. Then, at its tautest, it tore apart with a wet, squelching sound. Next came the dislocating of bone, fragment by splintered fragment. Each bone shard knit itself together again into a sleek patina of keratin smoothing the way down my vacuum mouth. Cosmic shanties gurgled from inside me, a litany of my own ancient ghosts.

And Thomae, intoxicated with gratitude, dived down the deep, dark tunnel of my throat.

How was I to know she would be rejected like a foreign body—she, who had been inside my mortal facade so many times before? Our essences prodding at each other, yet unable to truly mingle and integrate—oil and water. The terrors she met inside me—she, who always claimed to see the real me—changed her. I told myself her gift of the otherworldly would allow her to withstand the descent into primordial, unnameable things.

I plunged into my own being and bore witness to Thomae's transmutation inside me. How her eyes went gleaming with Understanding, then fever-bright as things she hadn't been created to comprehend, streamed inexorably inside her. She tried to claw her own eyeballs out, treading timeless, tenebrous seawater, choking on deep-space vibrations and laughter all the while.

With a roiling wave, I ejected Thomae from the vortex of my being. Yet the change in her lingered, as if parts of her had been remade or unlocked on a molecular level. Her quest for a Void to bury herself in, deepening still.

**

Sleep pulls like flesh hooks at my consciousness after I put the pinky away in the fridge. I manage to clean the spot of vomit and check on Thomae one final time. I should lie on our bed, but the heat emanating from her body overwhelms my senses. I collapse on the porch sofa instead. My vision blurs and my Void churns, disturbed by the earlier intrusion.

I dream of the forest overlaid atop the unfinished galaxy my monstrous kin and I once occupied. The rot and the moss where insects burrow the way we once burrowed through larval holes in the firmament. I can smell it, through human nose, insect proboscis. My monster siblings were there one day before time, and then they weren't—a vanishing act into my own maw. And though they writhed inside me—a lamentation of dark matter—I was still so empty. Still so hungry.

The insistent brush of fingers wrenches me away from the dream. I'm too disoriented to know if the touch belongs to the space that birthed me, or the encroaching forest. An unwieldy weight smothers my chest. Hands push against my collarbones, holding me down in clawed caress.

"Maria," a voice croons. "It's time."

"Thomae?" I try to sound through a parched throat. "What are you doing?"

"My love." Her bandages have come undone, dried blood and viscous pus anointing my exposed neck. "I told you before, didn't I? I have never found a lock I couldn't pick right open."

Iron-willed hands move from around my neck to hook into my mouth, slack with shock. Her fingers lodge themselves in the corners of my lips, her nails digging into the surrounding skin. The stump of her pinky drags bitter against my panicked, darting tongue.

Any other time, I would have been able to overpower her. Now, still heavy with the turmoil of my stomach and limp with her betrayal, all I can do is push weakly against her adrenaline-fueled strength.

"Thomae, it's me, what are you doing?" I try to say. But the more I open my mouth to speak, the harder she pushes—one hand forcing my upper mandible skyward, the other pulling my lower jaw into my chest. My words bleed together, then lose meaning altogether as my jaw unhinges against my will.

I lose control of my human corporation and the facade of normalcy I tried my hardest to maintain so I could spend more time by my lover's side. The same lover who now tears my face apart until my head is turned inside out and her laughter vibrates through my passageway, unfettered.

My sea of monsters, shipwrecks, and stars eddies with the sensation of Thomae climbing inside me. I can't tell if it's because of revulsion, or relish.

"Don't do this," I try to say. "You'll hurt yourself."

You're hurting me.

Thomae only cackles as she shimmies inside my mouth, feet-first. Her fervent body sears my gums, branding me from within. My teeth—a shifting amalgamation of human enamel, animal chitin, gas-giant hydrogen and helium—ache with the violation.

"You and I can rest at last," Thomae croons. "Like ferns in the forest, like snails in their shells."

I claw at her and try to pull her out, but by then it's too late. My fingers only extract a bloody fistful of hair as she slides wetly down the chasm of me. Once she's in my Void, I try once more to eject her like I did her pinky finger earlier today, and before that, her whole body. This time, Thomae is intimately familiar with the gargantuan waves battering her form. She knows how to resist, no matter how I heave and strive to abort her like a small universe of unfinished beasts.

I see you, she had told me once, and it's true. She's nested inside me before. Mapped out all my innermost secrets—things even I don't know, or am unready to face.

There can be no winner here. And still, my body fights her.

I don't generate tumorous eyes across my stomach lining this time. Cannot bear to watch the ravening. And still, I feel it from within—the way Thomae giggles, then sighs in relief as her skin bubbles and dissolves in my acid waves. I writhe and retch on the porch until there is nothing of her left. My lover absorbed the way I once absorbed my monstrous siblings in the nebular womb of the cosmos, forever stunting them into mindless, hungering things.

Thomae's liquescent bones sink as another shipwreck inside me. They, too, sediment at the bottom of my sea like silty sand and meteor dust.

***

I stay on the porch for a long time, until my face has regenerated gristle and tendon. The jaw bones have grown back crooked, unable to close all the way. I'm too lost in my stupor—my grief, her betrayal—to do anything about it.

Eventually, I dry my tears and drool, and go inside. The jar sits at the back of the fridge where I hid it to spare Thomae the heartbreak. Her mangled pinky finger, now my last keepsake. I stare at it like a saint's reliquary or a sinner's limb of glory. Was the Void inside me the only reason Thomae approached me in *La Belle et la Bête*? The beauty wanting me not in order to celebrate my monstrosity, but to exploit it? An escape from the perpetual stream of psychic power at first; later, a return to the vast fabric of the cosmos.

A doorway, she called me when we met. A means to an end.

I place the finger in my pocket, walk myself back to the porch where the song of bird and dawn beckons. And something more, a thrumming undercurrent that had shielded itself from me but for my most vivid of dreams.

I remember finding Thomae in the forest. The way she tried to bury herself there, after my body had rejected her. What did her naked-nerve powers sense among the foliage?

Perhaps the same force that summoned me to this nowhere town after I awoke from my centuries of hibernation.

Each of my unsteady steps down the porch creaks the water-damaged wood with foreboding finality. I might as well have been a corpse carrying several stones inside my sinking carcass. The firs resemble smeared inkblots across the horizon. The forest stretches silent. Yet when I blink down, my second set of eyelids kept hidden for too long, I trace the rumbling breaths of a sleeping, tree-clad beast. The forest, stirring at last.

It's not difficult to find the hole Thomae tried to bury herself in. Right there, under animal tracks and droppings, a wingspan of rain-rotten leaves. I kneel down and sweep my hands across the forest floor, revealing the gaping chasm. It appears too dark and deep to have been dug by Thomae alone. I stare into the hole. A fathomless, needful thing like me.

"Hello," I speak into it.

And the abyss echoes back, moist and primeval. "Hello, hello."

A call that thrums with ley line energy, dark-matter magic.

"Are you like me?" I ask through a scraped-raw throat.

And the hole, the forest, calls back, "Me, me."

I let my facade go. I had adopted it to blend with the humans. Gravitated toward *La Belle* and its glittering outsiders, hoping one of them would want to touch me long enough to make me real, contain me in my own shifting-galaxy skin. Thomae liked it when I shaped myself like a woman, body and face straight out of her favorite films. But right now I am monstrous. I'm featureless, and indistinct. Perhaps the closest to being me I have ever become.

I speak a name into the abyss, guttural and full of consonants. This name is not Maria, nor any word spoken by human tongue. It was the one thing I knew when I first came into existence. That, and hunger.

The forest, in a tongue just as ineffable, speaks its own name in turn. A series of sounds my Void recognizes before my ears do.

I was so ravenous when I was born out of nothing. No caretaker to gently touch and teach me my own borders, I stretched wide as a god or a universe with no end in sight. I ate and tore through everything in my path, including my own newborn kind.

Perhaps I was selfish in thinking Thomae and I could contain each other. She, cartographing my skin, and I, swallowing and soothing her. But the truth is, I wanted to taste her, too—have her fill the throbbing emptiness within. Now that I'm full, however, all I wish for is to be unburdened. To have someone else carry my weight for a while. Swallow me whole, make me a part of them so I won't have to pilot this hungering husk.

Perhaps someone like me. *Stronger* than me, like my kin that I never managed to destroy in our infancy. Cunning enough to conceal themself from my ravening ruin.

I speak my true name again, and the name of the ancient entity who has merged themself with the forest. Our two names resound together, the way they were once twined into the fabric of the universe.

I clutch my lover's last remnant in my fist and lean over the hole. Then I step inside like she did, feet first. This hole isn't sleek, but tenacious with mud and other effluvia.

I have to work my way in like a tunneling worm. I writhe while roots and thorns pull at my loose flaps of skin and clothing until I shed both of my cocoons. Where I'm going, I won't need them. The squirming insects eagerly accept my offering. They, too, must feed.

When the hole in the forest ensconces me, I pull moss and mulch over my head, eclipsing the rising sun. It hasn't been long since my last hibernation, but gas and dust of protostars swirl through my vision, calling for a return to larval state. Another drawn-out dormancy—a cradle of devolution for my weary bones—doesn't sound too bad.

I wait for my kin to reject me as a foreign body, but it appears we are compatible. Too evenly matched to dissolve or destroy each other in our boundless need.

"I've been waiting for you," the forest susurrates. "Why do you think I called you here? There's not many of our kind left. We should stick together."

I am sucked deeper into the forest's maw with relentless intent. Dirt gives way to the cool, velvet vastness of the cosmos—a familiar sensation against my legs now fusing into a vestigial comet's tail. Though my core still weeps like a lost child with Thomae's memory, the rest of my body erupts into song.

Carry me, unburden me, the song begs in timeless tongue.

The monstrous kin I once failed to devour is merciful as much as they are cunning.

I let them swallow me whole.

Sisters in Safe Deliverance

Lowry Poletti

In the woods on the Burnnet homestead, Frances and Covenance watch maidens bare their breasts and wail their laments. The warbling cries bounce from tree to tree.

Frances squeezes her sister's hand. Her own tears dried up yesterday, but Covenance sobs. Frances knows she should be here in the same way that she knew she should be at the funeral. The grave is only one day old. The maidens tear into the mound of sweet-smelling soil as if to pull Helen out from beneath.

There is something ancient about the maidens' mourning. Frances has seen it before in the maidens' lofty whispers, and in their cat-like poise and long tresses, but here she watches the undulations of a centuries-old beast with a dozen arms, legs and heads strewn across the ground. She's afraid if she lets go of Covenance's hand, she'll lose her sister to its maw.

Already, the girl's sobs echo the beast's cadence.

At the funeral yesterday, the village girls cried silently. They hid their faces behind black veils, and paid their respects in rose petals. The funeral was a civil, modern affair for men who called doctors in from the city and for daughters who never earned a spot at Helen Burnnet's heel.

"Covenance?" Frances says. She says it slowly. A jagged scar runs down the middle of her lip, and she's missing a chunk of her tongue. Even after years of healing, her new voice is still too big for her mouth.

"Mama said she wouldn't die," Covenance says. "She said the thing in her gut would become a worm first. That it would hatch."

"*Covs.*" Frances shakes her shoulder. "You should head back to the farm."

Covenance blinks and shivers like she always does when she comes out of a dream. "I'm sleeping here from now on." She was selected to be a maiden just a few days before Helen's death. Maidens sleep in the house.

Frances' nose wrinkles. "You absolutely are not."

"Mama said this is my home. She said barns are for animals."

Heat stirs in Frances' chest. By the hand, she pulls Covenance into the underbrush. There, she looks her in the eye.

"I just need to look around the house," Frances says. "I'm gonna clean it up for the two of us, and then we can stay there, okay?"

Covenance doesn't seem convinced, but she nods anyway.

***

The men and women of the village Safe Deliverance trusted Helen Burnnet with their most prized possessions—their daughters. The girls were brought to the homestead, and after five years, they were delivered as respectable ladies. Such rigorous tutelage left no space for nepotism, not even for one's own daughter.

The house is quieter than it has ever been, and so much larger, too, now that the maidens are gone. Almost enough space to breathe.

Frances lingers in the entryway, her hand still on the doorknob. A few days ago, the doctor asked Frances to witness Helen's death and sign next to his name on the Certificate of Expiration. Aghast that Frances had entered uninvited, Helen said:

Return to this place again at the cost of your life.

When Frances closes her eyes, she can still see that face wrinkled like the snout of a snarling dog, eyes wide and white, teeth clattering.

Mustering her courage, Frances checks each room. For valuables. For a deed. The whole place is exceedingly normal, and that sets Frances on edge. Helen is rotting. The house should rot, too.

Helen's death came quickly. *There was something growing inside of your mother,* he said. Perhaps it started the size of a pea, but it became so fat that she burst from the inside out.

As Frances runs her fingers over picture frames recently dusted and the herbs hanging over the kitchen window, the house seems to whisper: *Mother has just left to barter in town; in a few moments, she will return with a new hen bundled in her arms.* So Frances avoids the creaky floorboards like she used to do when she was little—a larval babe, sexless and inoffensive, always tangled between the feet of Helen's maidens.

In Helen's bedroom, the sheets are still wrinkled. Frances can't go inside.

Out of all the rooms, the cellar door is the only one locked. Puffing out her cheeks, Frances puts both hands on the knob and pulls uselessly.

Behind the door, nails click against the floor. The sound makes Frances go cold. She presses her ear against the door.

She hears: "Hello?"

It comes in a terrible whisper. Shrieking, Frances stumbles away.

"Oh, I'm sorry," the woman behind the door says. "I didn't mean to give you a fright."

Frances opens her mouth wordlessly.

"Are you still there, dear?"

The woman behind the door has a wavering, soft voice. Frances guesses that she must be a few years older than Helen was. She pictures a figure with big sad brown eyes, a little taller than her and a little wider, round-faced— really round, round as in lotus-leaf-round.

"I am," Frances stutters. "I'm sorry, I—why are you in the cellar?"

"Oh," she coos. "I'm just passing through."

"Who are you?"

A pause. The whisper of fabric against skin. Outside, the forest is so silent that the woman's breaths become the wind and her heartbeats, the pitter-patter of rain.

"You must be Helen's daughter," she says.

"No," Frances says. "I mean, yes, well—you're probably thinking of Covenance."

"No, Frances, I mean you."

Have they met? With a frown, Frances thinks that she would have remembered a woman like this.

"How do you know it's me?"

"You have such a lovely voice," the woman says. "How could I forget it?"

Frances swallows the saliva beneath her tongue. She wants to cry.

"I heard about your mother," the woman says. "I've been praying for you."

"Thank you," Frances squeaks.

"It was so hard when my mother died. There's chocolate in the jar by the hearth. It'll help."

"Thank you," Frances says, more easily this time.

"I hope you know that I understand." The woman lowers her voice, as if she's about to reveal a secret. With these few words, Frances draws closer to the door once again. "You can tell me. It's okay to feel relieved. Maybe a little happy, too."

Frances' next breath is a stab to the chest. "Who do you think you are?" she gasps. "She's *dead*."

"I knew Helen. She could be so unkind, even to her friends."

"No. No." Frances shakes her head frantically. "Who are you?"

"You don't remember me at all, do you?"

"You need to leave."

"Then open the door, dear." As the woman moves, her feet disturb the light trickling in beneath the door. "You must feel like an intruder here in this house that you so barely know. But a house without a woman is like a body without a heart. It's yours now. That's your right by blood. Open the door."

"I—"

Each word slithers out from the cracks in the wood: "*Open the door.*"

***

The sun sets. The maidens' voices have gone hoarse.

They try the door to the Burnnet house in vain. They want little else than to return to the breast of their matron, but they won't tear down the walls, nor break the windows, because they are too afraid of what they might find.

So they slink back to the village where they will sit at the doors of their parents' homes and scratch until they are invited inside.

Mother Burnnet never forbade them from leaving the homestead, but after just a few days nestled between the shoulders of their sisters, they never wanted to go.

Illuminated by candlelight, the maidens are ushered inside by their mothers. In their ragged clothes the older ones hide their familiars—dormice and bumblebees, and crows who understand the words of men.

These animals crawl between the floorboards, into cabinets, or back into the trees as the maidens' fingers are washed with leftover cooking water. There won't be enough to steal the soil from their skin, so their mothers promise to take them to the river in the morning.

Even beneath the grime, they glow—their hair made from brushed gold, their skin carved from marble. The maidens sit and they nod, but these houses are not their homes. They will sit, they will pretend, and they will wait for their youngest sister.

***

In the Millory barn, Frances mixes chocolate into two mugs of milk. As she does, she thinks about the woman in the cellar. She thinks about the woman's heart pulsing, hot and full of blood, at the center of the Burnnet house.

"I want honey in mine," Covenance says.

"We don't have any honey."

"Then I don't want it."

Frances clenches her jaw. She needs to be patient. Covenance was closer to Helen than she was. But it's hard, especially since she's been working longer hours for Miss Millory to feed the both of them. Years ago, when she fled Helen's grasp, she toiled from sunrise to sundown just to earn a bed here.

"I already mixed it up," Frances says, "You're going to waste all of this milk?"

"It's disgusting." Covenance makes gagging sounds. "I don't want it."

"*Fine.*" Frances knocks the mug off the table. It hits the ground so hard that Covenance yelps. "That chocolate was from Mama's house, you know. That's all she had left in the kitchen and now it's gone."

Frances trembles. It started after Helen selected Covenance to be a maiden. Frances has imagined her sister getting lost in the woods time and time again. Trapped between black boughs, Covenance falls into the jaws of a cougar who tears her limb from limb. After Frances imagines this, a deep shame fills her, but her blood rushes, too, like she's raced to the end of the market and beaten all the other kids.

But the barn returns to her: the kind eyes of the nanny goats and hay floating in the air and her sister sobbing on the floor.

"Fuck." Frances gets on the floor, too, and holds out a hand. "Hey. I'm sorry, okay?"

"You don't mean it."

"I do!" Frances draws a cross over her chest. "Swear on my heart."

A single wet eye stares at Frances. After a moment, Covenance takes Frances' hand. Together they share the same cup of chocolate and watch the hay soak up the spilled milk. The drink makes Frances think about the woman behind the door.

It's been a long while since she's had a friend.

"You know you're all I've got left." Frances lies, because she knows Covenance likes to feel special.

Covenance snorts, but she leans on Frances' shoulder anyway.

"Do you mind if I ask you about Mama?" Frances asks.

"I don't mind." But the question makes new tears run down Covenance's cheek.

Frances brushes them away. "We're still here, aren't we? You'll be okay."

Covenance's nod makes her black hair flutter. Frances adopted Helen's golden coloring, her olive skin and broad shoulders—and Covenance the rosy, pale face of their estranged father.

"What was she training you to do?"

The perfect maiden, and therefore the perfect wife according to Helen, is not servile, but essential; not pretty, but beguiling; not witty, but cunning. When she told men of her curriculum, she emphasized domestic practicality.

When she told mothers, she made it clear that *The Art* was a means to an end.

But Frances wants to know—what had they done to her sister, and how?

Covenance looks away. "I don't know. A lot of different things."

"Did you talk to the other maidens a lot?"

"Yeah," she says. She smiles dreamily. "They're all so pretty. And they sing, too. Do you think I can see them again?"

"They sing?"

"At night. Mama let me watch. We'd go out in the woods. Some of them were singing. Mama put a salve on Anna's face. When Mama wiped it off, Anna was beautiful underneath, like she was glowing."

It's not the first time Frances has heard something like this. Every few years, someone claims that Helen raises witches, that she learns her art from a demon in the woods. These rumors are short-lived. The nearby towns will trade gravid cows and white stallions for Safe Deliverance maidens, and who can resist the limpid eyes of one of those women?

"What do you mean?" Frances asks. "She had a different face?"

The look of wonder disappears. Covenance is bloodless.

"I'm sorry," she says, but Frances gets the sense that Covenance isn't talking to her. She sounds so frightened that Frances follows her gaze to the doors and expects to see a specter in the darkness beyond.

The eyes of a hare stare back at her.

"I'm not supposed to tell," Covenance says.

The fire ignites in Frances' chest again.

"Mama's dead," she spits. "You can do whatever the hell you want."

Covenance whimpers, but this time she juts out her chin. "You can't yell at me. I'll tell Miss Millory you hit me. She'll kick you out."

"*Try it*," Frances says. "Miss Millory isn't Helen."

***

Years ago, Frances sat in the meadow weaving a tapestry of flowers. She had a coterie of admirers, boys and girls who would dive into the woods for her and dig until their fingers went bloody.

Frances had learned early on that she needed only to ask, and the flowers would appear, no matter their cost. Her voice never worked on Helen, but there were so many other people besides Helen.

As she wove, one of her admirers returned, not with a bouquet, but with a headless chicken.

"It's for you," he said.

Frances was already suspicious. She'd seen her friends kissing when they thought their parents weren't around. She hated the sounds. She hated the smell of sex and how it stuck to the air for days afterward.

"My mom told me that when she was little," he continued, "they slaughtered a whole goat to celebrate a marriage."

Frances wiped her hands on her smock. "That's not a goat."

"Well I don't have any goats."

"We can't get married," Frances said. "We're too young."

"My mom got married when she was sixteen. That's not that much older than us."

Frances wanted to say *I don't want to marry you*, but admitting this would run him off forever.

"We just can't," she said. "Not yet."

"Can I kiss you, at least?"

She wrinkled her nose.

"I'll bring you another chicken."

"I don't want a chicken."

He had eyes like a dog. "What do you want?"

He always hung around another boy, a tall one with a mop of red hair and a lopsided smile. She could not use her voice to achieve his easy strength; even after weeks of practicing, she could not heave firewood over her shoulder like he did, or swing girls around by their waists as they danced. She hated how his face reminded her of what she may never have.

She said, "Kill your friend."

***

Before the night turns into morning, Frances returns to the cellar door.

"Hello?" she says. When she doesn't receive an answer, she knocks. The sound echoes.

"Will you tell me your name, miss?" she asks. "I just need someone to talk to. *Please?*"

She hates pleading. She never had to plead when she was a girl. With this new, hoarse, slurring voice, she has become a belly-up dog.

She turns her tongue, that bloated worm between her teeth, over in her mouth.

She knows why Covenance was chosen to be a maiden, and why she was not. When womanhood arrived for Covenance, she was pure of heart, mind, and body. When womanhood arrived for Frances, she was already broken.

Shaking, she digs her nails into the floorboards.

"Answer me!" she yells, but she doesn't wait for an answer.

In the shed, Helen kept an axe. Frances runs outside and returns with a white-knuckled grip around the handle. She strikes the door with a cry.

"Answer me!" Splinters fly into the air. With each creak, Frances imagines that the house has a mouth—open, gaping, crying.

"*Answer me!*" Axe abandoned, she rams her shoulder into the door. It yields, and she stumbles.

As the dust settles around her, she realizes that her lungs are burning and that her hands ache.

A staircase unfurls into the receding shadows.

Her body goes cold. She hugs herself before she descends.

Inside the cellar, shelves stand sentinel against the walls, holding rows of pickled roots, salted meats, and dried herbs. A knife, handle inlaid with carved jade, sits abandoned on the ground, but the green eye just below the blade stares in such a way that Frances is afraid to touch it.

Two stone statues—a hare and a butterfly—flank the bookshelf. Frances dares to open just one book. She can't read the words inside, but the swirling characters make her nauseous. It isn't English, nor Latin. Panting, she tosses it to the side.

Behind her, a drip echoes. Frances spins around. But there's nothing before her but a puddle in the grout.

She follows the drips upward. Suspended from the ceiling, a chrysalis weeps translucent mucus.

***

In the barn, a plate overflowing with fresh breads, cheeses, and strawberries sits in front of Covenance.

"What's that?" Frances asks, replacing one of the horses' tack.

She takes a moment to look at her sister—to really look at the soft black curls, the red cheeks, the green eyes. The soft sounds of Covenance's existence do nothing to fight back Frances' loneliness. If anything, her chest aches even worse.

"I went into town today." The words squeeze around mouthfuls of red pulp. Covenance drums her sticky fingers over a piece of parchment.

"Miss Millory won't house a thief," Frances says. "You need to take all of this back and hope the baker doesn't have his crop handy."

Covenance gasps. "I am *not* a thief."

"Then how much did you pay for this?"

"I just asked for it!"

Frances presses her lips together. She needs to be nice. Covenance is holding a telegram, and France won't know what it says unless Covs tells her.

215

But there's a twisting pain inside of her. She wants to fish Covenance's voice right out of her throat and swallow it whole.

"I don't wanna be here anyway," Covenance says. "Tell Miss Millory I stole it all. I'll live with Mama."

"C'mon Covs, I didn't mean it."

Covenance sniffs and stuffs a berry into her mouth. While she's placated, Frances sits behind her.

"What does it say?"

"You first," Covenance says. "How's the house?"

There's a splinter in Frances's palm, given to her by the axe's handle. It burns.

"I'm clearing out some junk from the cellar. There's mold and rotting things. Mama was storing old books where she wanted you to sleep, too. Now." Frances points to the telegram.

"It's from a friend of Mama's. Her name is Missus Eliza Rosen."

Frances bunches her skirt up in her fists.

"She says she lives in the city," Covenance continues, voice light. "And that she was one of Mama's students."

Frances imagines this sort of woman. Long gone are the days when Missus Rosen let her brushed curls tumble down her back like the village maidens; it sits in a beehive above her head like the drawings in the newspaper.

"What does she want?"

"She says Mama wrote to her right before—" Covenance stops and bites her lip. "She says that Mama wanted her to come here and help out at the house. She'll be here in less than a week."

"We don't need any help."

216

"But the ma—"

"Hey," Frances says, taking Covenance by the shoulders, "Forget about the maidens, Covs."

"Don't call me that!" Covenance spits. She slaps Frances's shocked hands away, her nails so long that she draws red marks across the skin.

With a gasp, Frances clutches her hands to her breast. Torn between shock and anger, she finds that fire has replaced the air in her lungs.

"It's for me, anyway," Covenance whispers. She holds the letter so tightly that it wrinkles beneath her fingers.

"What do you mean?"

"The letter is addressed to *me*." She shows her teeth. "Not you."

***

Frances' boy delivered a corpse to her favorite spot in the meadows. He brought it there at night, so no one would see, and he hid in the wheat grass, not sleeping, not eating, for a day and a half before Frances decided that it was a good time to make a bouquet.

The corpse smelled both sulfurous and sweet. Its belly swelled, and its skin was purple where it touched the ground.

When she saw how the glassy eyes bulged outward, Frances thought that, maybe, another person was inside of the corpse, using as a costume. She thought that their girth was making it split along the seams.

"It's for you," he said.

***

How is it fair at all? That Covenance has friends among Helen's friends, and that Frances has nothing but an empty cellar? Nothing but dust and bugs?

Frances stalks the Burnnet fields until she sees the cellar door through a window. The cellar must be below her now, in this place where the roses have outgrown their beds and Helen rots.

She presses her ear to the soil. Something beneath hums a melody.

Tears well up in her eyes. She digs her fingers into the earth.

"Welcome back, dear," the woman says.

"Where did you go?"

"Oh?" She pauses. "I wasn't gone long at all."

Inside of Frances, a taut thread snaps. She sobs, she laughs, and she sobs again.

"Oh dear, oh dear," the woman says, "I'm so terribly sorry. I didn't mean to upset you so."

Sucking in a breath, Frances stutters, "Are you back in the cellar? Can I see you?"

"Frances." The woman tuts. "Not yet."

"But when?"

Dewdrops from the roses dot Frances' face. She imagines the chrysalis, and thinks that she wants to touch it.

"You should know this, Frances," the woman says, "Helen cast you aside because she was afraid of you."

Frances shakes her head. "She wasn't afraid of anyone."

"Oh, she was. She was so deeply afraid, but most of all she was afraid that one of her daughters would usurp her."

"It wasn't me."

"If only I could show you! All the times I begged Helen to introduce us! All the times I pleaded with her to feed you, to make you fat with me, to leave this silly little place and become larger than ourselves!"

"She should have been afraid of Covs. She's everything I should have been."

"She seeks the same inheritance as you, doesn't she? Be wary of her."

"What do you mean?" Frances holds her breath, afraid that she may be heard by the other creatures that live beneath the ground. She's thought the very same thing, but it feels sacrilegious to hear it aloud.

The woman whispers, "She wants the house."

***

"You must understand," Helen said, standing over the corpse, "that this is your fault entirely."

Frances sat a few feet away from her, still holding the same flowers, crushed to pieces in her fists.

"You foolish, foolish girl." Helen paced the length of the body. She tasted the air. "What did you say to that boy? I can *smell* it. 'Go away. I hate you. Go kill yourself—I don't care.' You realize that you made this happen, yes? He's going to slit his own throat. Now you're alone, covered in someone else's blood and shit and piss."

A sob bubbled out of Frances' throat. In the second that her mouth was open, Helen yanked Frances' tongue

219

out. Metal flashed. With a scream, Frances tore herself away. Her face was wet and burning.

"You can't be trusted with that voice," Helen said. She tossed the knife back onto the corpse.

Frances tried to swallow, but the taste made her gag. It wasn't just blood in her mouth. She fell to all fours and coughed into the grass.

It tumbled out of her—a piece of her tongue, glittering wet.

Distantly, she heard herself. Moans fell out of her like a cow's bellows, and she snarled at this moaning, animal girl. *Stand up, bite her throat out, eat her.* But she could only cry.

When she looked up, there was Helen's face instead of the sky.

"Get on with it," Helen said. "Dig."

***

Frantic knocks float down to the cellar. Frances fears that the maidens have returned to claim the house, but when she goes to the front door, she finds her sister.

Covenance snarls and shakes the doorknob with the weight of her whole body. "You lied to me!" she shrieks.

"Covs!" Frances fumbles with the keys. "Calm down!"

As soon as it's unlocked, Covenance stalks inside, a black-haired whirlwind, and hooks her claws in Frances' blouse. Her face is swollen from crying.

"What the fuck is wrong with you?" Frances tries to push her away, but her grip is resolute. Fabric tears beneath her nails.

"*You lied!*"

Helen's curse echoes back to Frances: is this how she dies? Punished by her sister's hand?

"The maidens told me everything!" Covenance snaps upward. "They see you here at night. They can hear you!"

"Those bitches—"

"*You want to kill me?*" Voice low, Covenance's eyes become big green puddles, her lips blush soft. The mask is uncanny, as if she has become a doll. "I'm your only sister and you'd kill me? Over a *house*?"

"They're lying to—"

There's only one hand grabbing Frances' shirt now. Frances jumps away right before Covenance unsheathes her knife.

"You can't pull that shit with me!" Frances yells. "It doesn't work when I hate your fucking face."

Covenance grips the knife in both hands and grins with all her teeth.

Fear pangs in Frances' chest. The same fear she felt when Covenance grew four inches in one summer. When Covenance devoured a whole pheasant, bones and all, because her growing hungers wouldn't abate. When Covenance curled up in Helen's arms, their mother's narrowed eyes becoming wolf-yellow as soon as Frances appeared. The fear of becoming smaller than the one who came after—the fear of being replaced.

Covenance roars. When Frances ducks, the knife strikes the wall. A cloud of debris falls over her back.

She sprints down the hall as Covenance's footsteps thunder behind her.

In front of the cellar, the axe blade shimmers. Frances wraps her hands around the handle and growls as she pulls it free. A shadow falls over her.

Frances turns and swings.

She hits flesh, then bone. Each crack reverberates down the handle. She drops the axe when Covenance's shoulder collides with the wall and together they slide to the ground.

Covenance's eyes are still wide. She opens her mouth to speak, but her teeth are coated red.

"They'll know," she coughs out. "They're coming." When she breathes next, she shudders, then stills.

Shaking, Frances touches the wound. A shard of bone, protruding from Covenance's skin, reveals a layer of pink marrow.

"No." Frances groans. "No, no, no."

Stumbling forward, Frances pulls out the axe. The hole in Covenance's chest is black. Frances thinks that can stitch it back together again. She slides her hands inside, where she finds a bulbous sac and purple flesh that crumbles apart beneath her fingernails.

Frances forces herself to her feet.

She paces. If she burns down the house, no one will know. They'll bury the skeleton beside Helen.

She wipes her hands off on her skirts but nothing can rid her of the stain.

A flock of finches meet Frances's gaze through the window. She stops pacing. She knows who they are. She knows she needs to hide.

She takes Covenance in both arms and together, they go to the cellar.

Frances lays the body before the statues, then collapses beside it. Covenance's face looks like it's sleeping. A draft plays with her eyelashes; sweat shimmers on her brow.

Head hanging between her shoulders, Frances gasps for air.

Behind her, something squelches—the sound of fruit splitting apart. Barefooted footsteps whisper against the ground. Frances has to clench her jaw before she finds the courage to look over—by then, a slender hand reaches over her shoulder and flicks away the green remnants of the chrysalis. A coating of mucus makes the skin sticky and wet.

"Hush now." When the woman kneels behind Frances, her birth-wet wings fall to either side of them. The tendrils of her hair caress Frances' neck. "You will have everything you desire soon enough. Abundance, beauty—"

"My voice?" Frances whispers.

The woman laughs as she squeezes Frances by the middle. Then, she points.

Covenance's chest rises slowly. As fluid rattles in her chest, blood drips from her mouth. The woman palms the jade knife into Frances' hand.

"You're so close, Frances—" Lips to skin, she whispers. "—and I am so hungry."

Parts

G.B. Lindsey

"The third date is a good time to come clean," Evie said.

I straightened. A difficult thing, on this couch. I bought it to devour me while I devoured television. Sometimes a leg got caught and standing pitched me face first into the coffee table. The coffee table had vicious edges. The bruises never quite went away. "Ah. Skeletons."

Evie smiled politely. "No skeletons. And no closets, as you can see." She waved a hand between us, down my front, then down her front—a full, curvy front sheathed in patterned cotton. Long, red lily petals on black silk. Thick hair curled at her cheeks and her eyes were a rich, quicksand brown. Fragile skin, with veins so dark across the backs of her hands that I could map them. Her breasts were wonderfully shaped, one slightly larger than the other. Nothing like mine. The neck of her blouse arrowed between them, revealing freckled flesh and shadow. Her hips were wide and her legs opened just so. She made it impossible not to swallow.

"No closets." I risked a touch to her wrist where it rested on the cushion between us. Gooseflesh rushed right up her arm and under the sleeve of her blouse. Pebbles and pebbles. I longed to follow them, and could only hope my own body drew such attention, such a need to touch. I was

G.B. Lindsey

tall, with barely any meat on my bones. My breasts were smaller than hers, but they were nice. I thought they were nice. I'd chosen navy blue tonight with a high waist, and I wondered what she would think of the scars hiding beneath my dress. Would they disgust her? Might she trace them with her tongue? Her teeth? The thought ignited a razored and ravenous stretch inside, deeper than my stomach or my guts. Could she bring herself to bite along the keloid that blossomed beneath my navel, until the deadened flesh came alive again?

I touched it every morning in the shower, marveling at this numb, new lump of me. It was my other navel, a bulbous outie just below my innie. Two umbilical cords at once could do that. Some mornings, I fancied I'd been made of two people.

Others had words for the navel. *God, what is that? What happened to you?* As though I'd been stuck with a meat thermometer in the middle of a dark street, as though I'd chop it from my body if only I had the proper tools. But I liked to show it off, to lift my shirt and point, and watch their eyes skitter aside. And then come back. Their eyes always came back. They wanted to touch it, all of them, but never did.

Evie placed her hand—my God, was she reading my thoughts? I stared down at her fingers where they hovered above my belly. She did not quite touch. The urge to breathe, to inhale until my stomach met her thumb, was unbearable.

"Delia," she said, "I've wanted to tell you something. I've been waiting for the right time." A child's gladness curved her face. She touched down at last, her hand, my body. The famished feeling inched deeper. "Right before Thanksgiving, you gave your kidney to me."

226

I squirreled out of reach, up onto the arm of the couch.

She fidgeted, her shoulders stiff, then lifted the bottom hem of her blouse and pulled the waistband of her leggings down. There: a blade of darkened flesh arced down her side to just over her pelvis. Shiny staple scars lined it like alert sentinels. Months old—it looked the same age as my new navel, that same rubbery texture, that sheen. She ran her fingers along the scar tissue once, lingering, then lowered her shirt again and clasped both hands in her lap. Still, her fingers trembled and stretched in my direction.

For three weeks, she had waited to tell me. Three nights, three dinners, three greetings and three goodbyes. She had entered those bars and bistros, moved between all those people, those diners and servers, with a piece of me inside her, and no one had known. I had not seen it, but she had seen me.

The couch seemed very small, suddenly. I leaned backward.

"Please don't," she said. She inched forward and fell back again. Her hands wound tighter together. She had short, blunt, beautiful fingers. She reminded me of a puppy, ordered to sit but wriggling. "Please."

I dug my hands into my couch. A scent tugged, floral and fresh, new blooms in a newly turned garden. "How did you find me?"

The way her curls bobbed above reddening cheeks was riveting. "I had to look. You don't understand, Delia, I had to."

"Look at what?" I couldn't imagine. She was the recipient, and I was the donor. *Altruistic, non-directed.* There were several names for what I'd done, including *anonymous*. What had the transplant center given her that told her anything about me?

"I begged." She beseeched me with her eyes and her hands; even her body arched toward me as though I were the one drawing her in. But the smell of her had the stronger grip. My living room had never smelled as good as this. "They had to take my kidney out."

"Why?"

"It was enormous, and it had gone necrotic." Her shoulders lifted. "But it was a part of me and they took it away. Can you imagine?"

I could. They'd taken a part of me, too. But then, I'd offered.

"And getting a part of someone—a new, living part to replace the dead one... I had to, Delia. I asked Teri. Please don't look at me like that."

Teri. Teri, my transplant coordinator. The smile came more easily now. Alright. "It was supposed to be anonymous."

Her eyes lit. She inched forward again, but this time she didn't check it. "I know. I *know*, but I wanted to meet you. So badly. I wanted you to see all that you've done, all that you've—" She cradled her belly in her hands, then ran her palms fretfully up to her neckline and down to her thighs, watching them the whole way. "All you've given me."

What I'd given her was enthralling. She was the most exquisite woman I'd ever seen. Healthy and full, with nourished skin and radiant eyes. Her body was made to cup and to kiss, to worship, and instead she might have *died* before I ever laid eyes on her, rotting away with her rotten kidney. There was no place for such a cystic, festering lump beneath this flesh. Knowing a part of my body was in there instead, just inches away inside that perfect shell—

"I've scared you," she said.

"No." Fear was not what I was feeling. I summoned the truth from where I'd packed it away, next to that smoldering, hungry coal—what I'd prayed and prayed for but never confided to Teri during our many talks, never. "I wanted to meet you, too. To make sure you were right." *Young, intelligent, properly grateful. You'd owe me. You'd thank me every day and think of me every night. Your scar would be my name written across your skin.*

You'd use my kidney to save the world.

She smiled. Just dazzling. "Teri didn't want to say, at first."

"Well, she could get fired."

"She wasn't supposed to say, I know. But I persuaded her."

I laughed. Teri, with her apple cheeks and cheerful smile. I'd met her in person once, at the medical evaluation, and I'd known immediately that even if I could not choose who ultimately took it, my kidney was in good hands. Someone who loved her job, who celebrated it, who took it home with her.

You know what, Delia, I just love bringing people together! As many times as I do it... Well, there's nothing like that feeling. "Did you take her to dinner, too?"

Evie's smile dropped away. "I would never do that. Take her to dinner." The last part she muttered to herself, and she shook her head. The rest of her shook, too—the faintest vibration. It looked like my insides felt.

"I'm sorry." I hadn't meant to offend. I also hadn't wanted Evie and Teri to have three nights of their own. "How did you persuade her?"

Evie looked at me. *Always, please, always look at me.* "She didn't understand. She'd never given a part of herself up. She never took a part of someone else into her. She was a virgin, you know? I knew she was. I could tell. I don't mean of sex. She could never understand real virginity. No one can, until they lose it. Like I did. And you."

Two people, in each other. The image spread like light across my body and pooled behind my second navel. I pictured it piercing further, filling my kidney-shaped hole. I imagined a deeper closeness than that, and found nothing. I couldn't believe that Evie and I, such a short time ago, had been strangers.

"But when I finally got to see your picture," Evie said, "I think Teri felt it."

Polaroid. Quick snap, smiling at the doctor on the day I was cleared. Who still owned such a camera? Who had dug it from their attic, extracted it from their cellar? Who still knew what to do with it, now that it was out in the light? I remembered the flash in my face, the blink that rushed on its heels like the upswing of a heartbeat. What a day that had been. I'd wanted to give that kidney so badly, couldn't fathom why they were going to make me wait for three more weeks. They'd already taken too long, with their questions and concerns, their prodding and poking and examinations; my recipient was waiting, dying in tiny bits! How could they not understand? I'd called and called, and Teri had answered and answered. She'd walked me hand in hand right to the end.

But I knew Evie was right; Teri hadn't really understood. She loved her job, maybe even brought it home with her. But in the end, she did this for a living, and there were rules. Once, early on, I'd told her I couldn't allow my kidney to go to just anyone. No idiot kid, no distracted parent. No old person whose life was already over. Only someone who would celebrate their life, and mine. Someone who would honor such a sacrifice. Someone who would never forget, and who would make me glad.

But I'd heard it in Teri's voice. That *pause.*

"She told me what you asked," Evie said.

"She what?"

Evie's head dipped to one side. "What you asked. The eyes and nose. If you could even donate your feet."

My heart hopped, twice. "I never asked that." *Do people ever, you know.* We'd laughed, Teri and I, and I'd made it a joke, to keep from hearing that pause again. *Do they ever try to donate other things?*

"No," Evie conceded. "But that's what you meant."

I did? I *did.*

Teri, do people

Can I?

ever try to donate

One eye, one ear. Think of the toes!

limbs?

What might a wonder like Evie have done with my hand? If she had needed it—a car accident, perhaps, or an ugly, rapacious infection. The rot from her kidney, somehow risen to the surface and eating into that plump thumb, those lovely fingers. I let the fantasy play—Evie with my hand at her wrist. Evie, wiggling my fingers to see

231

how they moved. Evie, touching her scar with my hand. The image jarred; my hand would be a strange, strange addition to her body. It would give her nothing she did not already have.

But my insides had made her better. Just as I had told Teri they would.

"How is Teri doing?" For four months of tests and scans and phone calls, Teri wouldn't even tell me Evie's gender, but somehow, she'd told Evie everything.

Evie took my hand and pressed it just above her heart. I felt the warm, dense swell, and the breath she took that raised her flesh into the curve of my palm. A perfect fit.

"I brought her with me," Evie whispered, and tapped the back of my hand. "I brought her for you."

My ears hummed. Evie pulled at her blouse's neckline and dipped my fingers beneath. Her hand was so cold, the rest of her hot to the touch. I felt rough skin, lumpy and hard, little ridges dotting the top of her breast. The scar there was uneven, newer than the other. The stitching had been imprecise, an unpracticed hand.

"We two are so connected." Her voice rose to a delicate squeal of excitement. Blood darkened her cheeks to a rosy pink, and she licked her lips. "I felt it the moment I woke up, after the surgery. I saw you in my hospital room."

"They didn't let me into your room," I breathed. If only they had. If only I'd known where, I'd have crept in.

"All the same. I saw you there, next to my bed. I couldn't see your face, but your hand was on my incision. Like you were holding it closed. I didn't dare move. I lay there and I shook, I was so happy, and everything was warm. And when you walked into the bar that second night, I already knew it was you. I felt it."

"Second night?" I slid off the couch arm toward her. The bar had been the first night.

"Well." She smiled. "Our bodies had already met."

Yes, they had. Hers had opened up and swallowed a part of mine. The lily petals on her shirt were the same red as my carpet, and looked as deep and as lush; I thought I could run my fingers through them. My hand twitched beneath hers.

"So, I went to see Teri." She was still talking. "At her home. And then together, we found you, but it took weeks before we could meet you again. I had to rest. My stitches would have reopened. Teri would have fallen out." She rubbed my hand across the furrow on her breast, hypnotic. The scar bumped and dove under my fingertips, the hills and troughs of the heartbeat thrumming beneath. "I couldn't breathe with the waiting. You can't just get up and walk after something like that."

"No," I whispered, "you can't."

Which part of Teri was it? Which piece lay so close to Evie's beating heart?

"She brought us together," Evie whispered. "It was fair that she be part of it."

It was. Teri deserved that.

"Would you mind..." She edged closer, a ripple that started at her hips and drew her shoulders after them until she was almost against my side. The space between her stomach and mine buzzed. I imagined the hole under my navel reopening to meet the long hole in her flank. A different kind of kiss. "Would you mind terribly if I had the rest?"

"The rest?"

She trailed her fingers down my arm. Back up again. Patted twice. "Of you."

Oh. I laughed a little. Embarrassing, to misunderstand like that. My pulse dropped back to a steady thump, not helped by her hand—it made its way off my arm, across my side to my stomach, where it curled at the hollow of my belly like a fetus. Her thumb pressed, insistent, on my second navel. "Please. Whatever, whenever you want."

"Yes, but." She inched closer, as shy as a butterfly. Her fingers jumped against my belly. "Mightn't I open you up a little?"

A *very* different kind of kiss.

It comes down to this, my mind said to me, and sounded like Teri. *What do you want out of this relationship?*

"Open me up?" I felt dumb—a gaping fish lying across a plate, and she, selecting her silverware.

Open me. God, yes, with your fingers, with your tongue, with your hands and arms and eyes and teeth—

"Put the rest of you inside me." Her body vibrated again, as though there were a skin somewhere to be shed, and a new creature waiting beneath. She burned straight into me. "A little bit at a time." She wouldn't stop moving. I longed to grab her, to hold her in place where she belonged with our bare bellies touching. I wished I had not worn a dress. "Not all at once," she hurried, and took my face in her hands. Now her palms were hot and the heat of her bled into me. I could hear her heart pounding, beating against the part of Teri inside her and out to my ears. "Not all at once, just... you and me, coming together. Like we should always be."

"Always." I'd dig into myself if I could, pull it all out and offer it up. Oh, for *her*...

At the edges of her scar, the flesh was taut, a mouth pressed tightly closed. Holding its silence for just a little longer. I could tease that ragged line apart again and nestle a little of myself between her and Teri in that warm, wet, floral dark.

"I want you," she breathed against my mouth, "every part."

How might I taste, going down? Not through her mouth, but through the mouths of her incisions, the ones that existed and the ones...oh, the ones I had not yet seen and the ones we might make together. Opening her as the surgeons had opened the two of us in frigid, side-by-side operating rooms, and as she had now opened me. My parts, slipping one after another over a tongue of sinew and blood, of flesh and fat, and into the center of her for good.

I *starved*.

Under my hand, I felt the part of Teri, a firm nugget of tissue tucked against her sternum. Teri, who had first brought us together. Teri, in celebration. Part of one of her creations at last. Evie was right. It was beyond sensation.

I kissed her. I licked inside Evie as deeply as I could, and she licked me back.

She tasted like home.

The Court of Mouths

Cyrus Amelia Fisher

When I step into the preparation chamber to kill my wife again, she's eating a bar of soap. Her lips blister where the lye has touched it; her tongue will be worse, her throat a red ruin. Still she sits on the edge of the marble table, the grease cutter dimpling her naked thighs. She holds my gaze and sinks her teeth into the soap's waxy surface, staining it with her blood. Countless centuries of marriage, and we've not exhausted our well of pettiness.

"Immature," I say.

"Fuck you," she spits back.

The struggle that follows is pointless and humiliating, which is the sole kind of victory Adris is capable of now. Once she wielded the power of a feastmage; now we scrabble like children. I finally wrestle the bloody bar from her fingers, but not before she bites into the joint of my thumb and finger.

"This isn't productive," I say, binding my hand in a clean towel from beneath the sink. The tooth marks are smart with lye. Behind me, Adris's breath rasps in a ruined throat. When I turn around to push her back onto the slab, she goes without further complaint. Her skin is tacky, red with irritation; she's rubbed it onto as much of herself as she could reach. It will be a real challenge, to salvage something from this. I find myself almost looking forward to it.

237

"You know you can still end this." My fingers smooth away a smear of soap on her neck. "All Lord Thule asks is your apology, and your vow to serve him loyally. You'll hardly win his favor by insulting his palate."

"His favor?" Adris rasps. "Oh, darling. I think I can do without that for a while yet. Just look at what it's done to *you*."

In my way, I have always done the least harm I am able. I step behind her, my hands familiar as they pool at the juncture of jaw and throat so I can angle her the way I need. With one hand, I pull out my ubiquitous timepiece, and make a mental note. With the other, I slide the knife into the artery as neatly as a key into a lock, its point nuzzling past soap-smeared skin in a surge of blood. She barely makes a sound. I hold her in place as she dies.

In the silence and stillness of the aftermath, I begin my life's great work anew.

***

The kitchens beneath the Court of Mouths never cool, and never sleep. The great Lord Thule, where he sits in his high throne at the eternal banquet table, is ever in need of fresh dishes for his hunger—and so the feast goes on, demanding meat, tureens of soup, roasted tubers by the barrel and blood gravy to sweeten it all. The fae lords who sit at that table, day in and day out, eat slivers of candied lung off the sharp edges of daggers coated with tinctures to soften the constant threat of poison. The clang of their fists on the warped table boards ring down to the kitchens below, and there the lesser ones toil at our art.

As each course is finished, troops of gouge-eyed servants carry the ravished dishes to the kitchen's lowest realms. Here the bones are tipped into the sinkholes for the rats and roaches, the edible morsels salvaged by skeletal sous chefs.

I remember the taste of that hunger like a blade on my tongue. Since my promotion, I've been eating quite well. So do the blind servants and the chefs who have seen fit to bind a limb to the feasting table. Sentient flesh is a delicacy, after all, rich with the complexity of thought and feeling, the heady flavor of a mind. The flesh remembers. I know that better than any.

The largest platter is mine to scavenge. The bones lie scattered, many of them snapped so the marrow could be sucked. I dig through the tatters of flesh and teeth, the grisly chaos of a battle decisively won, until I find the bone I'm looking for. The first metacarpal, lying beneath an uneaten frond of garnish; I know it by the band of gold inland in the bone, and by the way it pulls me like a second sense of gravity. Thule will not commence a meal unless he can see it clearly displayed and can taste the familiar binding magic upon its gold.

I pluck it, slick with grease and gravy, from the remnants of gluttony and hold it in my fist. I carry it back to my kitchen like a saint's relic gaudied with gold. The rest gets tipped into the dark.

***

There is little warning before Lord Thule visits my workshop. One moment I am sharpening my knives, waiting for the moment in which the bone on the altar table becomes my wife again. In the next, I feel the swell of dread that accompanies his presence, as I hear the click of his claws descending the tunnels far above. I scarcely have time to swallow the tranquilizing draught which helps us lesser beings face the noxious glory of his presence. I keep my head bowed, spine straight and eyes fixed on my boots. To catch a glimpse of the feastlord is not forbidden, but it is liable to turn the stomach.

Hello, little butcher. His shadow falls over me, wide and writhing, his voice issuing from a dozen mouths. *How goes your craft?*

"Quite well, my lord." I incline my head. "You honor me with the trust of your feasting table."

Indeed, he hisses. *And you have adorned my table greatly, over the years. Your service pleases me greatly.*

"Thank you, my lord." I hesitate only briefly. "Was there something you wished to discuss?"

Yes, he hisses, long and thoughtful. *I must admit, I have begun to grow tired of the monotony of traitors' flesh. The meat has somewhat lost its savor. Perhaps the punishment has run its course.*

A traitorous flutter moves from my stomach to my chest. It has been a long time since I have felt that tender excitement, that precursor to relief. I can almost taste it on my tongue, like a packed sphere of sugar about to dissolve; perhaps it is finally over. I felt it during the morning that Adris and I attempted our escape, not knowing that within hours, I would be begging for Lord Thule's mercy and promising him an eternity of loyal service, Adris as rigid and unbent as iron beside me. She would rather die than beg—and so it fell to me to save her in the only way I could. Every stroke of my knife, every word of comfort bitten back, every spice and garnish and sauce. There can be no easy redemption, even now. She will be reinstated as a dish drudge, forced to work for decades to merely attain the position she spurned; but in time, it will come. Time has long been the only thing the two of us could be sure of together.

I will miss, I realize, the art we have created together. The symphony of muscle and sinew and spice. But to have her by my side rather than beneath my knife—yes, it is worth the sacrifice.

"Your judgments are ever just, my lord," I murmur. "I am certain that the traitor's blemishes of character have been purified by your noble digestion."

Yes, Lord Thule muses. His great bulk shifts around the room, segments curling and uncurling, hands slapping the floor where they emerge from pulsing flesh. *It was the suffering which gave the meat its succulence. A pity—I had thought to dine upon her folly for another century or more.*

The stillness which descends on me is far more profound than a lack of movement. "My lord?"

I'm finished with her, Lord Thule says. *Toss her relic into the vermin pits so they might be fed on her regenerating flesh. The roaches lack my discerning palate.*

Already I hear the chatter of the feastlord's great feelers tugging his body up the light shaft, towards the ever-dining court where even now his next meal awaits. Horror and disbelief freeze me in place, only my jaw wagging soundlessly as he withdraws. The last barb of his writhing tail has almost lifted from the floor.

"My lord—if you will. I have a proposal."

I hear the click of his claws pause on the stone walls gouged with marks. *I am listening, little chef.*

"Let me prepare a final feast," I say. I risk a glance upwards. His body is a shapeless backlit mass, hanging against the red light which filters down from above. Nausea rises; I hold firm. "As a celebration of your wisdom and

241

fair-handed punishment. Allow me this opportunity to redeem my craft in your eyes."

The shadow hangs suspended above, a dozen narrow claws and tendrils holding it in place. I have presumed too much. None but the lord himself may demand what dishes sit upon the altar of his table. Yet still I keep my eyes raised, though I feel tears gathering at my lashline and a throb in my left temple from regarding even the silhouette of his form.

Very well, he says. *But there will be a price. You will prepare the traitor one final time, and join me at the feasting table in one week's time.*

Then the Lord of the Feast claws his way back up into the upper echelon, eclipsing me entirely.

***

"Something's changed," Adris says on the third day. The blood-stained years have stripped us of our deceptions. She reads my tension in the grip I hold on my knife, the harried way I slit her throat the last two regenerations. This will be the third body laid out in the cooling room, awaiting my preparations. This meal, I can leave nothing to chance.

"Come on then," Adris says. "Did Lord Gut offer you a critique on the taste of my boiled sphincter?"

There's little use in keeping any of this a secret. "Thule is tiring of you," I say. "He has permitted me a single feast to change his mind, or else have your relic cast into the vermin pits."

"Ah. How grim." Naturally, she takes the potentiality of being eternally eaten alive by rats and cockroaches quite well. "I suppose your plan involves you cooking a meal so sumptuous and delicious that Lord Thule falls to his many-jointed knees in ecstasy, showers you with adoration, and promises to continue eating me for dinner for the rest of his unending existence. Placation is your signature dish, after all."

"This is no laughing matter." I pick up the knife, lift it to my whetstone rather than meet her gaze. "He'll destroy you, Adris." *He'll take you away from me.*

"He won't. If he does, he'll know I've finally won."

"You're mad if you think there's any version of this where you *win*." *Scrape, scrape.* My movements are practiced, but a fraction too fast. "He requested my presence at the feast."

I see the way Adris's body goes stiff. "What?"

"In seven days' time. I'll preside at the table when I present your final course."

A brief silence. I glance down from the knife to find Adris staring at me with an expression I hadn't seen in quite some time. I hadn't known she was still capable of fear.

"Pela," she says. It's a shock to hear that name, the private one she gave to me. Thule, who owns so much of me, does not even know it. "He's going to eat you. In case that wasn't imminently fucking obvious."

"Why would he do that?" The rasping whet of my knife to stone speeds up, battering back all doubt. "I have served faithfully. I have earned my forgiveness."

"You don't actually believe that." To my surprise, she sits up. "You can't attend that feast."

"I don't have a choice."

"Don't you? You're always saying how much more freedom you have. Now is the time to use it. Get out, flee, do what we were too foolish and weak to accomplish all those years ago. *Escape.*" She seizes my shoulders. I can scarcely recall the last time she touched me on her own accord in anything but violence. I stare into her eyes, inspecting the wildness there. Her desperation. I wonder how it will taste.

"I am going to save you."

She releases me with a sound of disgust.

Adris refuses to speak or meet my eye for the remainder of the preparations. When the time comes for me to wield the knife, my fingers tremble. Unacceptable. A knife requires precision, patience, and an understanding of the flesh deep beneath the surface so the cut will find its mark. I'd thought I had control.

"Just do it," Adris snaps. "It's not as if you have a choice."

She isn't wrong. My time frame is tight.

***

"This is how he does it."

Adris's voice is dull as she watches me secure the rope around her ankles. "He knows he can't break me, so he intends to kill you instead. It's the last piece of leverage he has left. And you're playing right into his hands."

I glance up at her. "A poor piece of leverage, it seems to me."

The silence spools out between us, as rough as the rope against my fingers. She doesn't deny it; I expected her to heartily agree.

"It may surprise you to learn that I don't actually want you to die."

"That's kind of you to say." I move on to the other ankle, making sure my knots are tight. "I suppose I've killed you too many times to say the feeling is mutual."

Adris snorts. It's been so long since I heard her laugh. It was her playfulness I fell in love with, so many years ago.

"I have a plan." I jerk the knots tight. "A solution that will preserve us both."

"I think I've quite had enough of being *preserved*."

"Trust me." I had not intended to speak those words; the sound of them surprises me. When Adris lifts her head to stare at me down the length of her body, her eyebrows are high.

"My dear Pela," she says. "Did you honestly just ask me that?"

"I don't expect it of you." I move a basin in the center of the floor. "I just want you to know that I'm asking."

She stares into my eyes a long while before letting her head fall back.

"I can't."

I don't blame her, and I don't ask again. So I set my strength to the winch until she's hanging like a tarot card, and the fingers I bury in her hair to pull her throat to my knife are gentle.

* * *

The regeneration happens with an almost anticlimactic quickness. One moment there's the bone, a yellowed nub on the white marble. Then, four and twenty hours after her heart beat its last, I will turn around and see her sitting before me as if my knife never once pierced her heart.

Always the same time frame—always from the moment I kill her.

Two days until I serve my final course. In the hours before her next return, I set to cooking. From the central kitchens I have requested a bounty of materials—fish and beef and partridge. I crush kingsfoil with the blade of my knife and reach for ingredients long untouched on their shelves. By the time she awakens, the air carries the rich tang of yak butter and early creamed yams, and the small table I have laid for her is ready.

She rises from the marble slab, her eyes dull as she inspects the miniature feast; when I pull out the chair for her, she goes without complaint.

"Fattening my liver?" she asks, scooping the first bite onto her fork.

I don't contest it. She shakes her head, and eats.

"I suppose this is the most I'll have to look forward to, if your plan works." She spears a potato whittled into the shape of a frog. "You might have cooked for me more often. I know I won't starve, but it's almost nice. In a sickening sort of way."

"I've strived to make your circumstances as tolerable as I was able."

"I daresay that's the most romantic sentiment you're capable of, darling." Her fork breaks apart the bright green skin of the fish before her, parting the razored scales I carefully dulled. "I suppose I'm supposed to finish all of this?"

"As much as you can."

It's a pleasure to watch her eat; to give *her* pleasure, in the one way I reliably can. It's been a long time since she had the opportunity to eat, and I can see the way enjoyment softens her brow and smooths out the lines around her mouth. I was never a particularly good wife to her. But at least I could cook.

"I'd give up, you know. If I thought it would save you." She drains the last of her wine and then looks at me, intent.

"It wouldn't."

She blinks. "I'm surprised to hear you say that."

"You were right all along." Every word is raw salt on my tongue. "And I was a fool, to think that I could sweeten the ocean with spoonfuls of honey. He has never intended to free you, nor to let me live."

The smile is gone now. She sets the wineglass down. "Bullshit."

"I failed you, Adris. And I can't ask for your forgiveness."

"*Bullshit.*" She stands, her eyes sparking. "Whatever this is, I'm done with it. I'd rather you use the knife—"

Her hand clatters on the table as she stumbles, catching herself; she stares at it in shock, and then raises her eyes to me. Then to the food. "Are you serious?" she says. "What is the goddamn point of going to all this effort just to poison me?"

"It's not to poison *you*." It's a presumption, but I stand to round the table and put a hand to her back, then clasping both her arms to lower her as she falls. She stares up at me, pissed off and then confused and then radiant with understanding—and then, it's just a seizure. Her lips foam red, her eyes roll back, and the elaborate, delicious horror I have lovingly cooked into every dish infuses itself into her flesh.

The moment she opens her eyes again, she's already grinning. "Fucking *finally*."

I incline my head, ever humble regarding my craft. "I am not blind to the fact that he will likely try to kill me."

"You'll poison him?"

"Doubtful," I reply. "You know as well as I, the devices he employs to avoid that. But I'd be a fool if I didn't at least attempt it."

She turns to the bodies, lined up against the wall. "What, then?" she murmurs, rising to go to them. I follow, my hands clasped behind my back. She inspects the first one, the salt-like crust on her corpse's skin.

"I wouldn't touch," I say, as she extends a finger. "The egg sacs are quite delicate."

"Gruesome," she says with approval. The next, I've threaded with the finest of razored fibers, enough to sever the tongue and jaw of any who sample it. The vat of blood I've mingled with salamander acid; the next is rich and fragrant, their terrible poisons hidden within her flesh. She stands before the row of dead selves, their faces crusted with rosemary and nightshade, deboned and marinating. Then she turns to me.

"You could have told me."

"You don't think he'd grow suspicious at the taste of triumph in your flesh?"

"Fair enough." She steps up to me. Her fingers touch my chest, just above the sternum. Tracing the loop of skin-warmed metal—hidden, I had thought, beneath my clothes.

"You still wear it."

I let her tug the chain free from my collar, revealing the golden band. I still remembered the moment of Lord Thule's sentencing, when we were dragged before him with the taste of freedom still on our lips; how he had forced her to perform the binding herself. The ring on her finger had begun to smoke, contracting through skin and tendon and flesh until it sealed itself onto the bone.

"I don't like to look at it," I say.

"You're disgustingly sentimental, beneath all the murder," she says, and pulls me in for the kind of kiss that shivers down every inch of my skin. I wonder, with the sharp-edged clarity that never fully goes away, how this will impact the taste of her flesh. I kiss her deeper. It has been so long since I was permitted to taste her.

***

On the seventh day, I ascend to the feasting room for the first and final time.

The main benches are empty, the tables bare; no guests will observe our battle tonight. Silence hangs thick in the high-vaulted room. The blinded servants fan out behind me, the great dishes hoisted on their shoulders. The air smells of spices and fat, and my wife's flesh cooked to perfection. For the first time in a long while, I let my uniform sleeves unroll to their full length past my fingertips. In the pocket of my chef's apron, I carry my knife and my timepiece. If I am to die, it will be with the tools of my trade with me.

The feasting hall's rafters bow like the inside of a ribcage. The smell pours over me in a torrent; my footsteps crunch as I make my way to the high table, bones cracking beneath my boots. The tables drip with grease and the rotting fragments of feasts long gone, mold fuzzing in the cracks of the wood, tendrils of slime wetting its underbelly.

A slow, cold horror rises in my throat. This is the altar upon which I sacrificed my great art? The smell is so overwhelming that it leaves no room for taste. I have spent hours carving shadowfruit into edible flowers, burning my fingers with its acid sap, to adorn a table crusted with refuse. I have poured years of my life perfecting the balance of salt and sugar for a meal on a bed of rot. I have made Adris's flesh into a masterpiece worthy of her death, serving it as ardently as any bridegroom—and then laid her down into a pig trough. All for nothing.

The high table sits above it all like a barricade against the filth. Tendrils of fungal growth creep flush with the elaborate carvings in its sturdy wooden legs. I ascend the steps, the dish-bearers laying the table ahead of me. Lord Thule sprawls across his throne, flailing legs and gnashing mouths from a hundred different anatomies. A single seat waits for me across from him, its back to the vast emptiness of the room. I sit. The dishes slide into place before us.

Welcome, butcher. Lord Thule's mandibles click in appreciation as he takes in the spread before us.

"My Lord." I bow, and then sit. "The feast is yours. All my greatest skill and effort, you see laid before you today. If I cannot please you with this, then my fate is in your hands."

Thule ignores me. His long, multi-jointed neck looms over the table, scanning the dishes. He finds what he is looking for at the center: a golden dish with seven metacarpal bones nestled within, the band of yellow magic glistening bright upon each one. Thule leans in close, inspecting them, his mandibles brushing the neat, boiled bones. All seven, all accounted for.

Good, he hisses. *Let us begin.*

No plate is placed before me; it is neither my honor nor duty to eat. I watch as Lord Thule reaches for the first dish. Upon it, Adris's body sits wreathed in a garnish of her braided, golden hair, frosted with salt crystals. Her roasted head sits in a wreath of roasted flesh, candied rubies for her eyes and apricots spiced with cumin stuffed in her mouth. Lord Thule selects a pale rib bone from the artistic carnage, sucking a tender glove of meat trembling on its end.

Ah... he sighs. His flesh trembles; my breath catches. *What a fine brace of poisons you've marinated this one in. I can say that for all the toxins I've sampled, I have never experienced so finely balanced a selection.*

My stomach knots. I bow my head, ever deferential. "Thank you, my lord," I say, swallowing my defeat. Six more courses. Six more chances.

He makes his way through my feast like an army pillaging a town. The soup he upends into his mouth, its acid splattering on his chitinous plates. He swallows the dumplings whole, scarcely grimacing as their poison bursts within his gullet. He picks the razored quills from a steak of Adris's thigh, mandibles sorting them from flesh as he eats, as neat as a weaver's fingers. The jellied brain cooked in basilisk venom nearly seems to freeze him, but with a shudder he swallows the final bite, and its petrifying poisons come to naught. He devours every crumb of every meal, flesh and bones crushed to meal in his jaws. He is weakened by the end—I can see it in the pained tilt of his long, segmented body—but it is not enough.

A fine attempt, he rumbles, pushing away the final dish and licking its grease from his multiple sets of lips. *The finest I have yet experienced. It will almost be a shame, little chef, to eat you for your arrogance.*

He rears up all at once, scales and plates and thrashing limbs rising like a column above me. The great, horrible reality of him is a throbbing pressure in my brain, a vessel longing to burst. I cannot look away.

"My lord, if you will. I propose one final wager." My voice shakes. He looms over me like a cresting wave over the table, a clicking mass of hunger.

You have nothing left to bargain with, little chef. His legs begin to carry him across the table, crushing dishes and snapping the remnants of bone.

"I have one." I brush back my long sleeves to lay my hands on the table, side by side. Thule did not ask to see them; there was no reason to. For the first time since the feast began, he stares down at them, the fingers narrow and dextrous, the bloodied bandage where my ring finger ought to be. The entire mass of him goes still.

It felt quite good to wear my wedding ring again. It hurt terribly, when Adris sliced the finger free; the binding spell had hurt even worse. There could be no room for doubt, no fake that would trick his perceptions. And so we made a new relic, bound in marriage gold, and I baked the last of hers into one of the dumplings.

The ticking of my timepiece fills the air. We had timed her last death so carefully.

"The remainder of my eternity, served on your table," I say. "Against her."

Lord Thule opens his mouth—and then convulses. A sound comes from inside of him like the tearing of wet cloth. His claws turn on himself, pawing at the layers of armor and beetle plate, the soft skin in between. He writhes, throwing his head back and falling onto the table, disturbing my wife's bones as he struggles. At once, his legs turn upon his own belly, digging and slicing until orange blood spurts in a mist. His screams shake the very air, echoing down to the thrum of the kitchens below.

And then, at last, he is still.

I surge forward from my chair, pulling free from the crust of filth that covers every surface in this place. My hand grasps weakly for the chef's knife on my belt, dabs it into the hissing acid which remains of the soup. Its blade smokes as I throw myself on the ruined gash that Lord Thule's claws made of his midsection, the tick of my timepiece in my ears. Pieces of plate peel away from the flesh, trailing sticky lines of tendon and gore. The relic bone—how long will the dead acids of his stomach preserve it?

The lingering poisons of Thule's flesh hiss on my skin as I cut, but there's too much flesh and I cannot let him consume her, not even one final time. I cut deeper. Inside, something is kicking with the weak struggles of a creature gone too long without air. The blade of my knife snaps with a sharp ring, brittle with acid and the force of my blows.

For a moment I stare at the maw of torn flesh before me and the tendrils of acidic smoke. Deeper within, the movements have gone still. Not much farther, now. I lean forward and begin to chew.

Acknowledgements

Thank you to lionheart, The Scary Stuff Podcast, Bridget D. Brave, and Cynthia Pelayo for their support of this anthology. Additionally, many thanks to all of our Kickstarter backers for helping to make this anthology possible!

Author Bios

Alex Luceli Jiménez

Alex Luceli Jiménez is a queer Mexican writer and high school community liaison living in Soledad, CA. Her fiction has appeared or is forthcoming in *Berkeley Fiction Review, Barren Magazine, Southwest Review,* and others. Currently, she is editing her first complete sapphic YA horror novel. She was born and raised in southern California. Tweet her @alexluceli and learn more about her work at alexlucelijimenez.com.

Ali Seay

Ali Seay lives in Baltimore with her family and a geriatric dachshund who rules the house. She's the author of *Go Down Hard* / Grindhouse Press and *To Offer Her Pleasure* / Weirdpunk Books. Her work can be found in numerous horror and crime anthologies. When not writing, she hunts vintage goods, rifles through used bookstores, and is always down for a road trip. For more info visit aliseay.com

Anastasia Dziekan

Anastasia Dziekan is an emerging queer American horror author. Her writing can also be found in the anthology *Nerve Janglers: Thirteen Tales of Terror.* A recent graduate of Ursinus College in Pennsylvania, Anastasia also enjoys stage magic, comic books, scary movies, and her two dogs. She has a passion for female representation in horror and an appreciation for the weird and wonderful.

Annabeth Leong

Annabeth Leong's writing has been recognized in a long list of best-of anthologies, including *Heiresses of Russ 2015: The Year's Best Lesbian Speculative Fiction, Superlative Speculative Erotica: The Best of Circlet Press 2012-2017* and several editions of *Best Lesbian Erotica*. She is the author of *Dark, Trembling Passion: Erotic Horror Shorts*.

Archita Mittra

Archita Mittra is a writer, editor, and artist, with a fondness for dark and fantastical things. Her work has appeared in Tor, Strange Horizons, Zooscape, Anathema Magazine, Hexagon, and elsewhere, and has been nominated for the Pushcart, best of the net, and other prizes. She completed her B. A. (2018) and M.A. (2020) in English Literature from Jadavpur University and has a Diploma in Multimedia and Animation from St. Xavier's College (2016). When she isn't writing speculative fiction or drawing fan art, she can be found playing indie games, making jewelry out of recycled materials, reading a dark fantasy novel, baking cakes, or deciding which new tarot deck to buy. She lives in Kolkata, India, with her family and rabbits.

Website: architamittra.wordpress.com

Twitter: @architamittra

Instagram: @architamittra

Avra Margariti

Avra Margariti is a queer author, Greek sea monster, and Rhysling-nominated poet with a fondness for the dark and the darling. Avra's work haunts publications such as *Vastarien, Asimov's, Liminality, Arsenika, The Future Fire, Space and Time, Eye to the Telescope,* and *Glittership.* "The Saint of Witches", Avra's debut collection of horror poetry, is available from Weasel Press. You can find Avra on twitter (@avramargariti).

Christina Ladd

Christina Ladd (she/her) is a writer, reviewer, and editor who lives in Minneapolis. She will eventually die crushed under a pile of books, but until then she survives on a worrisome amount of tea and pizza. You can find more of her work in *Vastarien, A Coup of Owls, Strange Horizons* and more, or on Twitter @OLaddieGirl.

Cyrus Amelia Fisher

After years of living all over the world and driving all over the United States in a beat-up minivan, Cyrus Amelia Fisher finally returned to the mossy fens of their birth. Now they while away the hours communing with their fungal hivemind and writing queer speculative fiction about body horror, haunted houses, and cannibalism. Naturally, they also love to cook. Find them on twitter at @hubristicfool.

E. F. Schraeder

E.F. Schraeder writes poetry and fiction that is most often inspired by not quite real worlds. The author of the lesbian gothic novella *Liar: Memoir of a Haunting* (Omnium Gatherum, 2021), which was an Imadjinn Award finalist in 2022 and the queer horror novella *As Fast as She Can* (Sirens Call Publications, 2022), Schraeder is also the author of a story collection, two poetry chapbooks, and other short work that has appeared in many journals and anthologies. E.F. Schraeder believes in ghosts, magic, and dogs.

G.B. Lindsey

G.B. Lindsey's most salacious and long-term affair is with the horror genre, but she also writes sci-fi, romance, and historical fiction. By day, she works in kidney transplant; by night, she sings, reads voraciously, and devours period dramas. She was recently published in Ghost Orchid Press's eco-horror anthology, *Chlorophobia*. You can find her works at www.gblindsey.com.

G.E. Woods

G.E. Woods (she/they) writes second world fantasy where marginalized identities are normalized and short fiction with whimsical rage. Her debut story appears in the bestselling all-trans and gnc-written new weird horror anthology *Your Body Is Not Your Body* (2022, Tenebrous Press). Beyond writing, she's a parent of goblin twins, dances under full moons, and talks to the trees near her home outside Chicago. Find her sometimes online via Instagram and Twitter: @gewoodswrites.

Hailey Piper

Hailey Piper is the 2x Bram Stoker Award-nominated author of *The Worm and His Kings, Queen of Teeth, Unfortunate Elements of My Anatomy, Your Mind Is a Terrible Thing,* and other horror books. She is a member of the Horror Writers Association, with over eighty short stories appearing in *Vastarien, Pseudopod, Dark Matter Magazine, Daily Science Fiction,* and other publications.

She lives with her wife in Maryland, where their paranormal research is classified. Find Hailey at https://www.haileypiper.com.

Twitter: https://twitter.com/HaileyPiperSays

Jade Lancaster

Jade Lancaster recently graduated from Durham University with a Masters degree in creative writing. As a queer woman of colour, she's looking to expand her insights and experiences through the lens of fiction. Jade currently lives in Northern England with her cat, Rupert, and finds inspiration in exploring quirky museums and antique bookshops.

Twitter: https://twitter.com/Jade__Lancaster

Kat Siddle

Kat Siddle is the woman you sit next to on the bus. She looks pleasant. Unthreatening. If you were looking closely, you might guess she was a librarian, but you're in a rush and not really paying attention. You notice, though, when she pulls out a laptop and starts typing. Why is she hitting the keys so hard? What is she laughing at? You glance at her screen. She's writing some kind of story. You read it over her shoulder. It's weird. You don't change seats, but you feel uncomfortable for the rest of the ride.

Lowry Poletti

Lowry Poletti is a Black author and veterinary student. When they aren't writing about monsters and the people who love them, they can be found wrist deep in a formalin-fixed lab specimen. Their other pieces appear in *Anathema*

Magazine and *LampLight Magazine*. You can find them on Twitter as @LowryFerretly.

Nicoletta Giuseffi

Nicoletta is a queer English language professor and princess under glass. Although she was born and currently resides in California, she left her heart in Hokkaido, where she taught in junior high schools. She is an advocate of decadence and cannot turn down a cake or a macaron even if she really wants to. Although she is currently querying a fantasy novel, she loves consuming and writing horror stories. Her passions include animal photography, retro games and hardware (ask her about her home office), and the late 18th century.

Twitter: @dearnicoletta

Rae Knowles

Rae Knowles is a queer woman who writes in South Florida alongside her Australian Shepard. She holds a BA in English Language and Literature with a minor in Creative Writing from Florida Gulf Coast University. This is her second publication. Her story, "The Last Self Portrait" appears in *Annus Horribilis* by Bag of Bones and she can be found on Twitter @_Rae_Knowles.

Tiffany Morris

Tiffany Morris is a Mi'kmaw/settler writer of speculative fiction and poetry from Kjipuktuk (Halifax), Nova Scotia. Her writing has appeared in *Nightmare*, *Uncanny*, and *Apex*. Her debut horror poetry collection *Elegies of Rotting*

Stars is forthcoming from Nictitating Books in 2022. Find her on Twitter @tiffmorris or at tiffmorris.com

Social media: Twitter @tiffmorris

IG: cryptidsarecute